THE
CONSPIRATORS

THE
CONSPIRATORS

A NOVEL

E.B. HENNING

TATE PUBLISHING
AND ENTERPRISES, LLC

Published by Tate Publishing & Enterprises, LLC
127 E. Trade Center Terrace | Mustang, Oklahoma 73064 USA
1.888.361.9473 | www.tatepublishing.com

Tate Publishing is committed to excellence in the publishing industry. The company reflects the philosophy established by the founders, based on Psalm 68:11,
"The Lord gave the word and great was the company of those who published it."

Book design copyright © 2014 by Tate Publishing, LLC. All rights reserved.
Cover design by Rtor Maghuyop
Interior design by Honeylette Pino

Published in the United States of America

ISBN: 978-1-63063-212-0
Fiction / Mystery & Detective / General
13.12.11

To RZH

My dear G—

Here it is, just as I promised—our story, as it began. I have excluded or altered the names of many of the dates and persons for the protection of all involved. There is no need, I think, of fear—it is safe now for the world to see and hear of the story that began our adventures.

As ever,

J

PART ONE

1

I begin my story on one of the nights that I walked alone down a familiar path, staring absently at my boots and disregarding the stars. I reflected upon the events of the day. I had been hassled and harried, and I kicked the gravel as I walked.

I shoved my hands deeply into the pockets of my coat and quickened my pace against the rising wind. Perhaps if I kept walking past my apartment, past this town, I could leave behind this body and molt, like a bird, into something better.

My boot caught on something and I stumbled a little. I grunted and kicked the shard in front of me, sending it skidding a few feet ahead. I stopped to examine it. I had tripped on the fragment of a statue, remnants of faded paint still forlornly visible on its surface, like the last bit of print on a newspaper as it burns away. I turned to see a large slab of concrete; the only part of the house once standing here that remained intact.

Mixed with dirt, rubble, and grime was the faintly discernable debris of a life that had once been rich and filled with texture and color, now lying in fragments on the ground. Only someone who had been part of the life here could recognize it now, could still hear the ring of voices echoing across the air. Soon no one would be able to recognize it at all, I thought.

A heavy weight settled on my chest. I felt my heart beat dully, reluctantly continuing in its inevitable rhythm. I heard a throttled groan escape my throat. I kicked the shard by my foot as violently as I could. I had walked the path to this plot of land more times than I could count. Each time I swore that I would never return.

I closed my eyes and breathed in deeply, feeling the sharp sting of the night air in my lungs, breathing it in greedily. I opened my eyes and began to turn away. Something cold and heavy hit the side of my head in a forceful blow. I heard the thud of my body as I hit the dense, cool dirt.

When I awoke, I was thirsty and my temples were pounding. I could not feel or see anything. I tried to move my arm, but it was held fast. I was bound to the chair, a blindfold over my eyes. I struggled against the rough rope stretched tightly across my chest and wrists, but I felt so weak that I soon gave it up. My face and arms burned. I could not move and could hardly breathe. A helpless panic rose in my chest. I was trapped and I had no idea why. An involuntary groan escaped my lips, resounding in the hollowness of the room.

"Hey, not so loud," a voice uttered urgently.

"Who's there?"

"It's me, the other captive," said the low voice. It was deep and forceful. I was dubious that another captive would address me so assuredly. I opened my mouth to respond but could not choose my words. Anything would do, really, but this situation was so beyond my capacity that I was baffled into silence. I tried to make sense of the situation.

"Where am I?" I asked at last.

"You're in a large, empty room in some sort of abandoned factory."

"But where?"

"Your guess is as good as mine."

"What's happening to us?"

"We've been kidnapped."

He said this with simple irony. He had assumed a familiar tone that seemed strangely fitting to our situation.

"How long was I out?"

"About a day and a half."

"How long have you been here?"

"Two days. I was only unconscious for a few hours."

"So you've just been…sitting here with me…while I was unconscious?"

"More or less."

I felt even more uncomfortable than I had before.

"You talked some in your sleep, so I got in a little conversation, but it's been pretty quiet so far. I was wondering when you were finally going to wake up."

"What did I say?"

"When?"

"In my sleep."

"Nothing interesting."

I wondered if that was true.

"Can you tell me a little bit about yourself? Maybe if we discover what we have in common, we can work out why we're here. Who are you?" All of these questions came quite rapidly.

"I'm Jack—John, that is, Westfield," I began, stammering. "I'm in graduate school. I work in a library. I don't think there's very much interesting about me, really."

I began fumbling around to see if I could find any of my possessions, my cell phone or wallet, something that might help me escape.

"Don't bother, they've taken everything," the voice informed me.

"Who? Who's taken everything?"

"Our captors," he said a little impatiently. "The only one I've met so far is Hart, but I know that he's part of some kind of organization. He keeps on mentioning someone named Fuller, and I think that's the leader of the gang."

He said all of this matter-of-factly. He seemed to have accepted as fact that we were captives tied up in an abandoned building, awaiting our fate. He also seemed to have decided that we were on familiar terms, comrades. This idea was comforting whether true or not, and I decided to assume it too, at least for the moment.

"Who are you?" I said after a moment's silence.

"Grey," he stated simply.

"Ah. And what is that you...did you...do? Before this?"

"I'm a graduate student in psychology. There's no reason at all why anyone should kidnap me. I'm not valuable."

He sighed.

"So, what's going to happen?" I asked after a long pause.

"I don't know," he said thoughtfully. "So far Hart has come in about four or five times a day to give me food and water, to make sure I haven't escaped. He seems nice enough but not quite dull-witted enough for my purposes."

He probably was not trying hard enough. I determined to demand our freedom as soon as Hart walked through the door.

"So you have no idea why you're here," I began again.

"On this Earth?"

"In this room."

"No idea."

"And you don't know when we're going to find out."

"Our next opportunity will be at approximately 6:45 p.m."

"Is that when Hart usually comes in?"

"As far as I can estimate, yes."

I sighed.

"They won't keep us here forever. At some point, they've got to either kill us, let us go, or tell us why we're here," said Grey.

"And which one do you think it'll be?"

"The last."

"Why?"

"It is unlikely that they will simply let us go. That would be useless. I can't think of anyone who would pay my ransom, so it is unlikely that they will kill us because of a failed ransom attempt. Therefore, I think it is most likely that they inform us of our purpose sooner or later."

"Well, I have my own purpose in mind," I informed him. "And this situation does not fit into it. I've been knocked unconscious, dragged to the middle of nowhere, tied to a chair, blindfolded, and I don't know about you, but this has thrown my plans into utter chaos."

I thought I could almost hear him smiling.

"Then perhaps you should make chaos a part of your plan."

A little while later, I heard a large metal door grate open. Grey and I sat in silence. My unanswered questions hung in the air. The only noise I could hear was the sound of determined footsteps proceeding slowly toward us. I felt my body shudder, and I tried to stifle the violence of the involuntary motion. The last thing I wanted was for my captor to observe my fear or to observe me at all. But I was exposed and vulnerable with nowhere to hide and nothing to do. I heard Grey's breathing growing a little quicker. I had not noticed it at all until now.

"How are you, Grey?" asked a resonant voice.

"I've had a comparatively pleasant day. How are you, Hart?"

"It's been a long day for me," said Hart in a strangely conversational tone.

"What time is it?" asked Grey.

"About 6:45."

I wondered if he was making a point to me.

"They sent me in to see if you'd be wanting a meal."

"Yes, we would."

Grey's voice was deep but clear and precise. There was no desperation in it, only steadiness and gravity that communicated a command of the situation he clearly lacked. He sounded, I thought, more like the host of a dinner party than a captive.

2

At the mention of a meal, I remembered again how hungry and unbearably thirsty I was. I could not remember what or when I had last eaten. Still, I did not want to interfere with the conversation, suspecting that Grey might have some kind of companionable influence with the captor that I lacked.

"We are wanting dinner," Grey answered in his firm, lighthearted voice.

"We?"

"Yes. He's awake now. See?"

"I do see," said Hart, sounding as though he were smiling.

"I envy you."

"I'll bring you dinner in a few minutes."

I heard rapidly retreating footsteps and the heavy door opening and closing once again. I writhed in my chair and turned my head as closely as I could to face the direction in which I guessed Grey was sitting.

"Did you know him before?"

"No, but I do now. He's the one who put a bag over my head. And he has spent two days watching me. It's part of his job. So we've had a bit of conversation, although my own thoughts often prove to be more entertaining than what he has to say."

I grunted.

"Will he untie our hands for dinner?"

"Yes, he'll untie our hands, but he won't take off our blindfolds."

After a pause, he asked, "Do people call you John or Jack?"

"Jack, generally, that's what my friends call me."

"And your family?"

"My family too."

It seemed impolite to ask him why he was called Grey, although he was not particularly bound to the rules of decorum, so we fell into silence again. The meal that followed was awkward due to the blindfolds, but I was so hungry that I hardly cared what I might be eating.

After the meal was over and Hart was gone, Grey told me the story of his kidnapping. It did not differ greatly from mine. Two nights ago, he had been locking up at the office where he worked part-time, and just as he got to his car door, a bag had been slipped over his head, and he had been hit with something just as I had.

"Two days ago," he said, "I was livid because the office had changed my hours so that I had to work more at night. And now I don't know if I will be alive in two days. Life is peculiar, isn't it?"

I did not know what to say to this. I wanted terribly to scratch my arm, but I could not figure out how to do it.

We spent the first part of the evening in silence, absorbed in our own thoughts. But as night began to deepen, we became aware of each other's presence and began to talk again. Our conversation consisted mostly in the questions Grey asked me, trying to discover a common connection between us. I tried to answer them as carefully and honestly as I could.

The first full conscious day of my captivity, Grey and I discussed the possibility of escape. The word, as I uttered it aloud, brought a strange sense of reality to our situation. It hung suspended in the air. I had said it quickly, but the weight of it brought a heavy atmosphere to the room.

"I don't think so," Grey said thoughtfully.

I attempted to shift impatiently in my chair, but my bonds quickly reminded me that adjusting my position was a luxury I was not allowed.

"Why?" I asked sharply.

"Well," Grey began slowly, "we do not yet know where we are or where we could go. Also, I don't think that our captors are planning to kill us. I think we are part of a bigger plan that we don't yet understand."

"I know," I said dismissively. "But if they are, in fact, planning to kill us, there's nothing to stop them."

I felt a pang of regret at the unintended hostility in my voice, but only a pang.

"Neither of us is worth a ransom as far as we can see," Grey began evenly. "I have no connections that would make it worth anybody's while to use me as incentive for money."

"Right, but maybe our captors just don't know that yet, and what do you think they'll do when they find out?"

I knew that they, whoever they were, did not want me for any benefit they could gain from my connections. I was nobody. It was, in fact, very unlikely that anyone would notice my absence.

"Before now," I said, thinking aloud, "I've enjoyed my solitude. I've reveled in my freedom."

"Certainly."

"But in reality, it's been years since I've spent as much time with anyone as I'm spending with you now, and that's only because I can't leave."

"I'm flattered."

"I've been proud of my solitude. It's been an asset and a tool. Now it's being used against me as a weapon."

He assented with his silence.

It struck me for the first time that it was just faintly, insanely possible that this was not an arbitrary kidnapping as I had presupposed it to be. Perhaps the people holding us in captivity had chosen me for the very reason that nobody would miss me.

As the end of the second day of our captivity drew near, I began to dread the oncoming night. In my blindfold, it was always dark, but there was a kind of density to the darkness of the night that was inescapable, palpable even beneath the blindfold. It is this kind of darkness that a child cannot escape when he pulls the bedding over his head in terror. Children instinctively sense and acknowledge the terror that waits in the dark. In the darkness of night, a panic warded off during the day creeps into the soul, and deep, long-standing fears come dreadfully to life.

For a child, this fear takes the form of monsters and ghosts—gruesome and fantastical things crafted by a distraught imagination. But as the child begins to grow up, the fear takes a more real and terrible shape; doubt, self-loathing, and regret haunt him and cause him panicked, sleepless nights that he puts behind him in the morning and tries to forget. He reassures himself that he can get through another day. If he is lucky enough, he even forgets about the terror of the night, but how long is it before he goes to battle with his doubt again? Is it the thoughts that arise at night that reveal his true self to him? Was he only consoling himself with foolish comforts during the day?

During the first conscious night of my captivity, I found little relief from my distress. Now my doubts, fears, and regrets haunted me in the liveliest fashion.

My determination to escape was weakened by Grey's words, but it strengthened at the thought, imaginary as it might be, that there could be people looking for me. I was angry because I could not reconcile myself to forming a plan of solitary escape. But surely he could fend for himself. Surely I could not be expected to stay here idly, awaiting my own fate alongside him.

Question after question echoed in the vast, empty silence of my brain, betraying me through weary wakefulness. I could make no headway. Slowly, my thoughts drifted farther and farther away from my current circumstances to a more general review of my life so far. I was twenty-three. I had hardly lived any of my life at all. I was full of intentions for my future.

———◆◆◆———

When I was a little boy, I spent most of my time with my head full of notions of adventure. My early intention for a career was to be a pirate, which I believe is not uncommon among boys of a certain age and disposition. I had a penchant for mischief and thievery and had a useful, but harmless, stash of delightful items in my tree house. I had an idyllic childhood. I tasted fresh air every day and romped and splashed to my heart's content. I got into the sort of trouble that seemed dangerous in my mind but which always resolved in the warmth of the kitchen with a clean bandage on my knee. I had nothing to fear, and I regarded the world with confidence.

It was during my thirteenth year that my fortunes changed. I experienced the moment that occurs too often in young people's lives, when the world was turned upside down, and I realized for the first time that all was not as it should be, that the world was a cruel and frightening place, where seemingly arbitrary elements fell together to lead up to one disastrous event that destroyed the world as it was before.

I came home from school one crisp winter afternoon and wondered why my neighbors were in our kitchen alone. Mrs. Wilson was sitting at the kitchen table, her face in her hands, heaving with inaudible sobs. Mr. Wilson was standing at the kitchen counter, very tall and straight, but with his hands pressed in fists against the counter so hard that the knuckles were white. He turned when he heard the door shut behind me, and I saw the strained, compassionate, yet profoundly uncomfortable look in his eyes.

I cannot recount the exact words he used to communicate to me that both of my parents had died in a car accident that day because I cannot recall them. I cannot recall hearing them or responding to them. I only remember turning and running back out through the door and through the heavy snow, tearing against its resistance. I remember climbing into the tree house and sitting motionless in it for the entire afternoon, letting the news and the cold numb my being from the inside out.

I remember noticing that the laces on my left boot had come untied and thinking that I should tie them but deciding I would not. I remember the unbearable sunlight shining coldly and mercilessly down on me and the unreasonable hatred at nature itself that swelled up in me, at the sunlight exposing me so heartlessly to the sight of the world, at the birds so thoughtlessly and cheerfully singing in the winter air, and at the cold—the cold that had made the snow and the ice that covered the road and caused a stranger's car to swerve out of its lane and into the side of my parents' car, which spun off the road, ending their lives and destroying my world in one brief, irreversible moment.

So many things cannot be undone. So many mistakes cannot be unmade. It is these things that haunt our nightmares and wake us in the dark.

I felt the tears soak my blindfold. I was grateful for the dark for a moment, if only to conceal my pain, to hide me from the world, to stop the moments and events long enough for me to breathe out a silent sob and remember the dreadful days of the past.

I remember that it was not until the dark had descended on me in my tree house that I considered anything other than the one truth that I could not comprehend. As the chill in my bones caused me to shake, I remembered my little sister and wondered whether she was in the house. I did not remember seeing her go in. I climbed down the tree but lost my footing in the dark, and when I fell, my face was cut by one of the stepping-stones leading to the tree, leaving me with a visible scar from that dreadful day.

I walked slowly to the house, remembering my legs, my arms, the backpack that had sat on my back all afternoon. I twisted the knob to my front door, which was so carefully locked by my father every night, but that now swung open silently and easily. I kicked the door gently closed behind me and dropped my backpack on the floor, feeling strangely light once it was gone from my back. As I began to walk away, I suddenly remembered to turn and lock the front door myself. I padded quietly up the stairs to the door of my sister's bedroom, cracking it slightly open.

I entered my sister's bedroom and crawled onto the bed beside her. She was asleep, and I lay next to her on my back, staring at the ceiling. There I lay for the duration of the night, pondering all of the implications of the events of the day.

Some days slip by without any notice, coming and passing almost without detection. But every now and then, a day comes along that changes everything, whether to increase fortune or to turn the world upside down.

When the relief of morning finally came, my desire to escape was renewed with even more intensity. I felt that if I did not get up from this chair and take off this blindfold soon, I would begin to go insane. I did not know what time it was or if Grey was awake so I sat quietly for what I guessed to be about half an hour, listening to myself breathe slowly in and out, then when I could bear the solitude no longer...

"Grey," I pronounced into the void.

"John," came the reply.

"We've got to get out of here today."

"How do you suggest we do that?"

I had thought this through while I waited for him to awaken, so I began quickly. "We'll plan a word signal, and when Hart comes in to feed us breakfast and untie our hands, we'll grab the butter knives. One of us will give the signal, and we'll slit the ropes around our waists, take off our blindfolds, and make a run for it."

"Where would we go?"

"Anywhere."

"What if Hart has a gun?"

"We'll just have to risk it."

"What if the door is locked?"

"Windows."

"No windows?"

I had no answer. Grey was quiet, leaving my proposal suspended in space, sounding unconvincing. I squirmed in my chair, waiting for him to say no, growing more irritated by the second.

"Well, if you don't want to try to escape, I can do it on my own."

"I think," Grey iterated slowly, "that we should wait a little longer before we try to escape."

"Why?" I asked angrily. "What are we waiting for?"

He paused.

"For the right moment."

"That will never come."

"It will come when we choose it."

"We've got to choose it soon."

"Just wait...a little while longer."

He sounded so confident, so unafraid. It irritated me. Why was he not as desperate to escape as I was? He sounded so sure of himself that I trusted him, even while wondering whether or not I ought. Reluctant and somewhat surprised at myself, I agreed.

"All right. We will give it one more day. But if nothing has happened by tomorrow afternoon, we've got to try something. Agreed?"

"Agreed."

3

At what I judged to be about eight in the morning, the heavy door opened and Hart thudded across the room. Twice a day, he took Grey, then me, to a cramped, grimy washroom just at the end of a hall past the large metal doors. Once inside, I could wrench off my blindfold for a moment, but there was only a dull light bulb inside and no windows, so I remained practically blind.

When I was ready to return to captivity, I put my blindfold back on and knocked on the inside of the door, and Hart opened it, ready with my wrist rope again. For me, this event was the worst moment of the day. The near freedom was excruciating. I dreaded it. Even more, I dreaded the short time that Grey was gone. I hated being alone in the room, blind inside my own head, wondering if Grey really would come back.

I heard Hart untie Grey's hands, and he gave a quiet but sharp intake of breath. I listened to the unnatural shuffling of his feet as he crossed the floor away from me, led by Hart, attempting to sense his way. I felt a strange tightness rise in my chest as I heard the two of them pass through the door on the far side of the room.

Only a few minutes had passed when I head the door open again.

"I miss seeing the moon," Grey was saying conversationally, which seemed to be part of his method for interacting with his captor. "The moon inspires me, you know. I could rest content for another three days if only I could see the moon for an hour."

Hart did not respond, but there seemed to be a companionable silence subsisting between them. I could not understand Grey's willingness to piffle with our captor, as if the perpetrator were really likely to sympathize with the plight of the victim.

"When do these blindfolds come off for good?" I asked abruptly as Hart began to untie my wrists.

He did not respond. The silence between us was far from companionable. We made our journey to and from the end of the hall in hostile silence. When I was safely tied to my chair again and I had listened to Hart's footsteps receding from the room and the heavy slam of the door, I felt a tense silence settle.

"You are angry with me," Grey said, bemused.

"No."

"Yes."

"Well, yes, if you must know. You are trying to befriend our captor and charm him into letting us go!"

"And you are trying to bully him into letting us go."

"Do you really think your plan is going to work? He probably doesn't have much of the control, you know. What do you expect to gain by winning him over?"

"What do you expect to gain by frightening him?"

"Information."

"Influence."

"That's hardly logical," I accused, beginning to be flustered. "A criminal like that isn't going to respond to witty conversation."

"But he is going to respond to your demands?"

"What is your plan, really?"

"What makes you think I have a plan?"

"Well, you keep asking me to wait."

I thought I could hear him smiling.

"But today," I continued, "something has got to happen."

"Or what?"

"Or we have to try to escape."

We sank into a frustrated silence.

I must have drifted into sleep because I was jerked awake by the slam of the door and the sound of purposeful footsteps proceeding toward us. I could hear the sound of Grey being untied and shoved toward the door. Before I had time to say anything, the door had slammed again, and I was alone. I began to panic. Had his plan worked? Perhaps they were finally calling him to his fate. A thousand thoughts passed through my head during the few minutes that went by before the door opened again. I heard a hurry of footsteps approaching me. It was not Hart; of that I was certain.

I felt cool, strong fingers slide beneath the ropes on my arms and a sudden release as the ropes were loosened, then I felt my waist released, and before I could reach for my blindfold, he had grasped both my wrists and was quickly leading me toward the door.

I did not resist. I felt no doubt that it was Grey leading me, and I did not question it. I allowed myself to be led through the door, feeling my own feet shuffle uncertainly across the still unfamiliar surface, my legs feeling weak and unsteady from hours of inertia.

"We are coming up on some steps," he whispered. I reached for my blindfold just as he whispered, "Don't take off your blindfold yet."

"How…why are we doing this?" I finally asked in a low voice.

"Don't worry. It's all right. Just pick up your feet, one by one. There you go," he said quickly, not answering my question.

I stumbled two or three times as we ascended what seemed like hundreds of steps, but we finally reached the top. Grey let go of my wrists for a moment and with a grunt of great effort, pushed open another door, grabbed one of my wrists, and guided me through. The door closed dully behind me, and my senses were overwhelmed by a sensation I had not felt in an eternity. It was a breeze—a cool, fresh, tantalizing breeze—sweeping around me and through me, stirring my hair and lifting my spirits. I felt Grey's quick fingers undoing the knot of my blindfold and, as it fell away, I gave an inadvertent gasp of pain and pleasure.

I was beholding the night sky. It was that dark shade that cannot be just black but a converging of purple and blue. The stars were bright, pure points of light that kept the sky from billowing all around us, and the moon— the moon was indescribably bright. I turned to Grey, seized with a violent curiosity about his appearance.

He was facing away from me, looking out over the railing of the rooftop toward the moon. He had a long, lean white face with distinctive features that gave him the air of an intellectual. He had high cheekbones and dark hair that looked rather long and unkempt, probably due to his days of captivity. He was taller than I and slender. His clothes, like his hair, were dark and disheveled. Suddenly he turned upon me with a keen gaze. He was young, I realized, perhaps even younger than I, yet there was something dark and enigmatic about him that made him look serious, perhaps something about the expression in his eyes.

Grey and I did not talk much. We simply stood in the cold darkness of the night and looked at the sky and at the world far away beneath us. We were in a city as I could tell from the dim glint of streetlights, but it was unfamiliar and shrouded in fog. It was clear that there was no hope of escape from where we stood. As I turned at last from staring bleakly downward to try to catch a glimpse of some distinguishing feature of the city, I saw that Grey was watching me with a peculiar expression in his eyes.

"It seems that our adventure is quickly coming to a crux," he said.

"An end, I hope," I replied.

The corner of his mouth barely curved into a smile, but a spark in his eyes betrayed him.

"You don't want it to end then?"

He looked out at the moon again.

"No."

"Well, it is most likely you who will get your wish," I said, hoping I was wrong. He turned and looked at me again.

"Perhaps."

We then stood silently for the better part of an hour before Hart retrieved us, and we descended back to the large, nearly empty storage room that had composed our cage for the last three days.

"Something is going to happen today. I'm sure of it."

"Of course you are," I said. It was the morning after our night of freedom, and my spirits were low.

"They let us take off our blindfolds yesterday," Grey said in his matter-of-fact tone. "That indicates that something is going to happen soon, surely."

"That means that now we can watch each other wriggling around in our ropes."

"Well, if I'm wrong, we can always enact your inspired plan of escape."

I did not reply.

"You know, you look just like I thought you would."

"How so?"

"Oh, you know," he began vaguely. "The untidy hair, the worn-out shoes, and—"

"My hair untidy?" I interrupted. "Have you seen yourself lately?"

"No," he said wryly.

"And what do my worn out shoes say about me?"

He laughed to himself. I waited impatiently, eyebrows raised, ready to protest.

"You feel misunderstood," he began carelessly. "Because you are, perhaps," he added before I could interrupt. "People misunderstand you. And you let them stay in the dark because you like being misunderstood. You have an intelligent face, but you're very prosaic. You like concrete facts, which was clear from the beginning. You don't like to say what you think, but you will if pressed. Mostly you like to observe people, perhaps even critique them. You probably don't think a lot of people worth your time."

He paused. I did not say anything. I felt supremely uncomfortable and irritated. I wondered how long he had been working all this out. I did not like being observed. I was used to being misunderstood or ignored, and perhaps I did rather like it, but I did not like having it pointed out to me. Grey was looking at me expectantly.

"Are you waiting for me to tell you whether you're right?"

"Of course not, I know I am."

"Well, if you are, perhaps it's because you recognize your own flaws."

"Perhaps I do," he replied disinterestedly.

Once I had seen Grey, the thought of securing my own freedom at the disregard or expense of his was out of the question. Nothing in his speech or manner suggested that he needed my help, and I was careful not to betray my decision. Perhaps I could still convince him to try to escape with me. Perhaps I could not.

4

At what I judged to be about 10:00 a.m., we heard the familiar entrance of Hart.

"Good morning," Grey greeted him. I said nothing.

"Yes, it is," Hart replied. "Today is going to be a bit different for you two."

"How so?" I interjected, unable to restrain my impatience.

"You're going to talk to Dr. Fuller today," he replied, saying the name reverently.

Grey was right. I anticipated the change with a shock of excitement and anxiety. No matter how unpleasant the revelation might prove to be, I felt I was ready for it.

My idleness had developed in me a confidence in courage that was probably unwarranted, but I was convinced of my ability to handle the encounter we were about to face. If Fuller simply shot me, it could be no worse than my continued captivity, I thought.

"When do we go in?" I asked.

"Just the one. You'll be going in separately."

I felt a lurch in my stomach and my confidence fading. I was profoundly uncomfortable at the thought of being separated from Grey. I dreaded the thought of being ushered into a room alone with a stranger. Still more, I dreaded waiting alone in this room, speculating about Grey's fate and waiting for his return. But it was worse than useless to protest, so I acquiesced with my silence.

As I had feared, Grey was the first to be escorted from the room, and I thought I could fume in solitude, but Hart retuned in a few moments, and I simply sat in silence. After a while, I began to shuffle my feet together and apart rhythmically, a hostage habit I had developed when the silence threatened my sanity. A tune started itself up in my head to the rhythm of my feet, and I occupied myself with it for a while. I began wondering what kind of questions I could ask Hart to gain some information.

Hart was a bulky, rather dull-looking man, red and clumsy, who looked more like a government worker than a kidnapper. I amused myself with speculations about his background. The hostility stood between us like a wall, and we remained on opposite sides of it, as unreachable to each other as if the wall were made of brick. I allowed my thoughts to wander, which was a rare pleasure for me now. I spent most of my mental energy pondering our prospects of escape.

I had come to fear the uncontrollable facets of mental escape, for I would just be brought back abruptly to the reality of my captivity. I had found that there was an intellectual danger to wandering thoughts just as there is a physical danger to wandering feet.

When Grey was finally brought back to the room, I had no time to question him. My blindfold was shoved back over my eyes, and I was roughly compelled through the door. I stumbled down an unknown corridor, suppressing a feeling of panic as a hundred new thoughts, dreadful and immediate, crowded urgently into my brain, each trampling the other. I did not know what kind of surface I was walking on now. The worst kind of fear was sharpening my terror every instant.

A door opened. I felt carpet beneath my feet. Carpet had the familiarity of a distant memory; the feel of it, the way it changed the smell of the room, made me nostalgic for something long forgotten. The strange shift to a more comfortable, familiar environment shocked me, and when I felt myself let down into what I could only take to be an armchair, I was surprised at my subsiding fear. I wondered if I should be afraid of the subsiding. This sensation did not last long, however, for when I heard a new voice, I adjusted instantly back into sharp awareness.

"Good morning, Mr. Westfield."

"Good morning."

"My name is Daniel Fuller."

I waited for him to continue, not knowing what to say since he already knew my name.

"Mr. Westfield," he began again, "I am meeting with you today to tell you about a project for which you have been selected. I need hardly explain that it is highly confidential and that your participation is vital. Therefore, your response is crucial and your secrecy required."

"My response?" I repeated. "I thought all my decisions were being made for me now." I felt my courage returning.

"Far from it," Fuller responded gravely, unruffled. "Up until now, of course, your participation has been compulsory."

I snorted derisively, but he continued. "But that is going to end today. Your response to the information I give you will be entirely according to your own judgment. We will, of course, monitor your response and see to it that you don't put our operation in danger, but refusal is an option. In that sense, it is we who will now be at your mercy."

"In that case," I said, "I would like to make a request."

"Yes?" The man paused his monologue.

"I would like you to remove my blindfold. I have no intention of striking any kind of deal with a man I've never seen. You have, at present, every advantage over me. I would rather we both have our vision. Does that seem reasonable?"

There was a slight pause, and the knot behind my head was loosened. I was now both untied and restored to vision. I looked around me and gave myself a moment to take in my surroundings. I was in an office, dimly lit but orderly. It was the kind of room that palpitated with secrecy—not in the sterile, rigid way associated with federal investigations and governmental conspiracy, but in the organic, living breathing way associated with the cosmos—the secrets of the trees or of the universe. Immediately, I sensed that I had been drawn into something large and continuous like the night sky—something that had been going on above and beneath me my whole life.

Perhaps it was only the half-lucid fantasy of someone emerging from darkness, but every line, every contour of the design of the room seemed filled with a rich, tangible meaning. I took in the dark wood of the shelves and the desk, the subtle arch of the ceiling, and the sense of vigor and motion that came from the papers and pens, organized but fully functional and ready for use—everything part of something active and energetic but immersed within the dead walls of a forgotten structure where no one would think to find it.

I looked around me slowly and deliberately, taking in every aspect and detail of the room as if through the lens of a camera. I refrained from looking at my companion until the last moment. It was an unconscious impulse I suppose, whether because I was nerving myself for the encounter or simply postponing it. Anyone else who had been in the room was gone now, and I finally summoned the courage to look at the man opposite me.

He sat in his chair, his arms resting on the desk in front of him and his hands folded. His attire was more scholarly than business-like. He had coarse, well-combed brown hair flecked with silver and calm, deeply set brown eyes. They were the kind of eyes that spoke of experience—hardships, conflicts, losses—the kind of eyes that seemed capable of both deep compassion and profound judgment.

I was intimidated by those eyes but somehow stirred and inspired at the sight of them. I was not intimidated because of the power and control possessed by this man, although I might well have been, but because I felt myself inexplicably desiring to win his approval. The moment I saw his eyes, I wanted them to look on me with approbation, as if I were a son seeking the approving glance of his father.

"Mr. Westfield," Fuller began in an even tone, "You have been chosen for an important, complicated, and dangerous mission."

I wondered if I was supposed to respond. I had nothing to say.

"I cannot describe exactly what you will be doing. That you can only discover for yourself. I can only tell you what we hope to send you into and what your objective would be. I will be giving you a dangerous amount of information here in this room because there is no other way for you to make a decision, no more effective means of persuasion. However, if you decide within the next twenty-four hours that you do not want to be involved, you will be allowed to walk away from the mission."

This statement seemed incongruous to me. That these people, whoever they were, had gone to the trouble of kidnapping me, concealing me, and holding me against my will, and now that this man was offering to give me a dangerous amount of information and allow me to walk away was incredible.

"Why can't I walk away right now?"

"Because you have been chosen, John. We have compelled you this far for a reason, but we will compel you no further. If you decide that you want no part in this mission, we will return you unharmed to the life you were living before. But if, after hearing what I have to say and taking the time to consider it, you decide that you want to accept the mission, well then, you will have to see it through to the end."

5

Fuller paused and looked at me tenuously. I closed my eyes and breathed in as deeply as I could, trying to absorb the gravity of the impending moment. In the short moment of silence, I braced myself for whatever might come.

"I am going to tell you about a group of people, a secret society you might say," Fuller began. He paused, looking at me with a peculiar expression on his face.

"It began with a rich, young, and radical man. He was clever, well-educated, and continually supplied with every opportunity and resource he could desire. He had a lot of time at his disposal."

"And his name was?"

"Felix."

Fuller reached out and straightened one of the pens on his desk with a small, precise movement.

"Felix's adventures began in earnest when he decided to pull a clever prank on a lawyer in his father's company. Felix had known this lawyer for a long time. The man had been over for business meetings and dinner parties throughout Felix's adolescent years. But before you understand the significance of this prank, I must go back even farther.

"As I said before, Felix was very bright and his family very wealthy. Naturally, his education reflected this. When Felix went to college, he developed a reputation for being rash and irresponsible and for living the reckless, careless life of many of his age and class. But Felix also fell in love. He met a girl named Alexis, almost exactly his opposite, and some said his affection for her began to reform him. But when the two eventually became engaged, Alexis's father objected to the match, well aware of Felix's reputation. Alexis would not disobey her father and the engagement was broken off.

"Everyone expected Felix, young and passionate, to become violently outraged and to use his father's influence to try to regain Alexis's hand. But he surprised everyone by continuing his reform even more drastically, devoting himself to his studies, withdrawing into near seclusion, and becoming a focused, studious intellectual. He dropped nearly all of his former antics."

"To win her back?"

"No, and that was the other surprise. He never spoke to her again. Felix got his PhD, joined his father's company, developed a new and respectable set of friends, and inherited his father's mansion after his father fell ill and died. Felix became one of the most respected and influential men in the country.

"Felix was always eccentric though. He began a tradition of inviting eight students from around the country to his mansion for a lengthy stay each year, always young, bright, and clever students like he had been. It is considered a great honor to be chosen in his annual invitation."

"What about Alexis's father?" I interrupted, "Is he the man Felix pulled the prank on?"

"Yes," Fuller smiled wryly, "I was coming to that.

"It took a long time to put the pieces of the story together, even for us. All we knew was that twenty-one years ago, Alexis's father was charged with embezzlement from Felix's father's company and sent to prison. It was Felix, in fact, who helped him to get out of prison after the crisis, but his reputation and career were effectually ruined. Because he was found guilty, not much research was devoted to discovering the circumstances surrounding his crime. As I said, it took us years to discover exactly what happened.

"I'll sum it up this way: Alexis's father had been on the verge of financial ruin. He had lost a vital case and several of his investments had failed. Felix's father's company was threatening to fire him. Some of the extended members of his family had lost their money too and were unable to repay money he had lent them. Suddenly, he had found himself with access to an obscure fund in the company that was virtually forgotten. When we finally traced back all the steps of all the elements, we found Felix himself. Without doing anything illegal, and hardly anything even traceable, Felix had engineered the details of the situation to present Alexis's father with the opportunity of saving himself through this one wrong, illegal act.

"Even if we presented our evidence, which for many reasons we are incapable of doing, it would hardly implicate Felix. Any and all of the details could have been purely coincidental and were certainly perfectly legal."

"So he got his revenge," I said, trying to grasp the meaning behind this strange story and its possible connection to me.

"More than that," Fuller said gravely. "Felix did not choose this form of attack by accident. He had witnessed many delicate conversations between his father and Alexis's in his youth. He knew the details of the financial situation because his father was preparing him to join the company. He knew the details of Alexis's family's situation because she had told him herself. Most importantly, he could access and manipulate Alexis's father's weaknesses in a way that no one else could. He knew of his financial anxiety, his concern about providing for his family, his pride and unwillingness to be in debt or ask for money. He knew even, perhaps, of a slight inclination to greed. He studied the details for both the man and the circumstances and manipulated to set him up for the ultimate temptation."

"He played devil's advocate."

"He played the devil."

"How do you know all this? How do you know him so well? You said it was almost impossible to trace. How could you know his motives like that?"

"How I know is immaterial. What is important is for you to understand the seriousness and complexity of the situation you could be entering."

"So," I said, beginning to understand, "this wasn't Felix's last adventure, was it?"

"No, it was only the beginning. After Felix discovered his power and the pleasure and secrecy of his revenge, he began to indulge in schemes like this on a yearly basis."

"His annual invitation…" It was beginning to become clear.

"Yes, his annual invitation. Eight young, promising students come to stay for a visit in the mansion and together they enact a complex, sophisticated, and untraceable scheme. Playing the devil as I said. And every year, they succeed with flawless accuracy. No one can ever trace the yearly gatherings to the yearly scandals. There are, of course, rumors about the secret society, but they are never confirmed. We are powerless to stop them. Our only hope is to infiltrate the society and discover the inner workings of one of their schemes. The scheme changes every year. The group almost completely changes, and the likelihood is that no individual member of any of the past groups has quite enough information to help us, even if they were willing."

"So that is where I come in."

I could see it now. With a sickening knot in my stomach, I began to connect everything and realize what Fuller was about to say.

"Yes, we want you and Grey to be part of their secret society. However, you will not be involved directly with the scheme. Only four of the students are directly involved with different pieces of the scheme each year. The other four are given the same set of information and go through the same set of instructions as the other four members. It's like being an understudy. This system is Felix's way of insuring that nothing can go wrong because if anything happens with any one member of the team, another member with the same, incomplete set of knowledge and tasks is there to take his place. You and Grey are going to be two of the understudies. That is," he added, "if you accept the mission."

"So our job will be to trail one member of this secret society and discover what their role is and report it back to you?" I was trying to comprehend it, my mind whirring.

"More importantly than that, your job will be to discover the scheme they are planning and stop it before it happens."

"But how can we do that if we aren't given enough information to understand the whole plan?"

"That's why we're sending in two of you," said Fuller. "That way, you can compare notes and perhaps help us put together the whole story."

"Who are you?" I asked at last. "What is this group of people you seem to be leading and why are you trying to stop this other secret society? How do I know that it is you who are in the right? For all I know, you could be the villain."

Fuller smiled. "I could be."

6

Fuller paused and gazed at me, then said slowly, "We are a secret society, yes, underground, unofficial."

"Working with the government?"

"Not so much with it as *for* it."

"And does anyone know you're working for it?"

"As I said before, we cannot bring Felix to justice in the typical way because we have not yet found any evidence of directly illegal activity. We are going to have to penetrate their defenses in a more psychological manner."

Fuller stood up and walked over to a bookshelf. He gazed at the books on it for some time. Without looking at me, he said, "This is a subtle, more complicated war than you can imagine. These people are the product of a social class that has come to believe that they can reinterpret morality or discard it altogether, that they can manipulate people's choices of right and wrong through their wealth and whims. The young students have been indoctrinated into the belief that what they are doing is ultimately for the good of humanity even though it is often a direct result of personal vendettas. More importantly, they have been indoctrinated into the belief that they are entitled to the results they wish to achieve, no matter what means they might use to achieve them."

"And you expect me to persuade them otherwise?"

"Not persuade them, thwart them."

"In other words, to achieve *your* results by whatever means possible?"

"John," Fuller said, crossing the room and leaning toward me over the desk, "these people are criminals. Their crimes are nuanced, varied, and precise. They are utterly without morals or responsibility. They have got to be stopped."

"And I am supposed to stop them?"

"You are supposed to become one of them. The physical infiltration of their society will be the easiest part. We have everything set up for you. You have no anonymity to protect because you will be known as yourself. You have come from high society just like the rest of them, and you are a bright, well-educated student. You are a perfect match for this role. Yet you are relatively unconnected.

"No one you know has any idea where you are, and you yourself could have given no hint of your disappearance or destination since you were not aware of it yourself. That is why we removed you the way we did. But you are going to have to penetrate their system on a psychological level. You will need to learn to think like them. You will bring any information you gather to us. In the end, you will do whatever it takes to stop their scheme before it comes to fruition and they damage even more lives."

I thought about how Fuller and his society had damaged my life and felt my anger rise.

"Why did you choose me?" I asked. "How do you know that I am not the same?"

"Have you spent a penny of your inheritance yet?"

I made no response. I had no idea where he had gotten all his information, but I was certainly not going to give him more. He smiled.

"You could have been living extravagantly all this time, yet you are working in a library to pay your way through graduate school."

"That doesn't mean that I'm the hero that you seem to think."

"But you could be."

There was silence for a few moments. Fuller looked at me almost compassionately. But he only said in a quiet tone that warded off protest, "You don't need to know right now exactly why you were chosen, John. In fact, knowing why you and Grey in particular have been chosen would only hinder your purpose at present. All you need to know is that you *have* been chosen for this task. I have chosen you. Now you must decide what to do."

"Didn't you decide that for me when you took me hostage? Won't you have to kill me or wash my brain or something if I refuse?"

He sighed and put his hand over his eyes for a moment.

"We would have to require your secrecy, yes. But we would not kill you."

Somehow I suspected there would be more to their request than a solemn swear of secrecy.

"You are irreplaceable, John. Consider this task with a careful mind before you reject it."

I only told him, "I will."

Slowly, I stood up out of the chair. I walked out of Fuller's office no longer blindfolded and no longer tied and found Hart outside the door. I followed him down a dim hallway and up to the large, metal door that I knew to be the doors to the room where I had spent the past few days. It seemed that I was once again in control of my own destiny.

Grey was walking slowly around the periphery of the room, gazing at the objects around him with a look of sober concentration. He looked up when I came in, and we stood for a few moments at the opposite ends of the room, gazing at each other in silence. I heard the door close behind me, and we were alone. I breathed in deeply and looked around the room. I saw the chairs in the center of the room with our severed ropes lying beside them. The room was large and dim with high ceilings, cold floors, and colorless walls. There were a few tables, chairs, and other items fallen into disuse, lying around the room, looking faded and forgotten. It was a strange contrast to the room I had just left.

I thought back to everything Fuller told me about Felix, about our mission, about his strange hope in me. I looked at Grey and wondered what he was thinking. There was no sound left in the room except for the quiet pulse of our breathing. At last I simply asked, "What now?"

Grey looked at me thoughtfully, smiling faintly.

"You were right," I said. "We were brought here for a purpose."

He nodded.

"A crazy one."

He nodded again.

"They're going to let us walk away if we want."

Grey looked at the ceiling and did not respond.

"Grey," I began again, "you're not considering this, are you?"

He looked down at me, and I saw instantly the answer in his eyes.

"I am."

"These people kidnapped us," I spat out harshly. "They kidnapped us, and they've been holding us hostage for days. Now they want us to infiltrate some kind of secret society, gather information for them, and try to thwart a scheme that we will never completely understand. It is insane."

I could not even find the words to describe how insane it was. I spluttered for an explanation.

"It is extraordinary," said Grey with what sounded like disguised delight. I began to walk across the room toward him.

"Given the opportunity to walk away from a situation like this, how could you consider doing anything else?" I asked. He turned to examine a table that was standing next to him.

"You can't do this," I said with earnest desperation.

"Why?" he said, suddenly looking up, his eyes flashing dangerously. "Why can't I? Because it's insane? That's hardly for you to judge."

"It's dangerous," I began again, trying to speak slowly, still advancing toward him.

"Hardly a reason."

"What possible—"

"And *you!*" he interrupted. "You ask how I could consider doing anything but walk away! Well, I ask you, how could you not consider a chance to do something actually heroic given the opportunity? Is that not less honorable, even if it is more safe?"

"What possible reason could you have for wanting to do this?"

"You are only thinking from your own perspective," he accused, facing me now.

"What other perspective is there?" I cried.

"Maybe you're right," Grey said, walking away from me a little. "Maybe this is some kind of insane mission or crazy trap or something and these people are out to hurt us for some reason and we should get out while we can."

"Right—"

"But what then?" he continued rapidly, suddenly spinning around and walking toward me again.

"What happens after we go home?"

"If they let us—"

"Yes, yes, if they let us. Then what? We carry around this secret with us for the rest our lives, of being given a secret mission to stop criminals and walking away. How does this have any significance if we don't see it through? Will it just become an unfortunate incident we survived and left behind us and tried never to think of again?"

"And what of it does?" My voice was rising. "What if we do return to our lives and carry this secret with us? I don't need this to have significance. It happened, and that is enough."

"What if they do need us, John?" he said, standing very still and looking at me steadily, our eyes meeting. "They knew what they were doing when they chose us. Surely you have seen that. Maybe we really are the only ones who can help them."

"They still haven't explained why it's us!" I almost shouted. "They still haven't explained that. We have no reason to trust them."

"They could have killed us a long time ago."

"And that's your reason?"

"No."

"Then what is it?"

"What if everything they told us is true and we walk away?" He looked at me with absolute seriousness. "Most people wait their whole lives for a chance to do something heroic, and it never comes. Haven't you ever wondered if you'd have the courage? Are you telling me that you don't?"

I was very close to him now. I could see that he was breathless and flushed. He began speaking more quickly.

"Everyone hopes to do something important, to change the world, to influence humanity. People talk that kind of nonsense all the time. Now we have a real chance, probably our only chance. We've been thrust into it without warning, yes, but now we've got to decide. This is our chance to have a radical effect on the world. Do you really want to just give it up?"

"We don't even know if we're really going to do something important," I said feebly, my voice lowering now. "We may just end up getting killed, or it may all come to nothing. Do you really want to risk the rest of your life for this? For a moment of heroism?"

"Do you really want to live the rest of your life without it?"

He came a little closer to me, and I looked at his face. I saw a look of passion, pain, and distress. It unnerved me.

"Why do you feel that you have to do this?" I asked.

"I don't feel. I think."

"What is that makes you *think* you have to do this?"

"My humanity," he replied, not breaking my gaze. "I could not wish that anyone would walk away from a task like this, so I cannot, in good conscience, turn my back on it."

"So you are really going to do this?" I said in a low voice. He nodded.

The horizon that had opened up before me when Fuller told me that I could be a free man was quickly shrinking, about to disappear. I felt tightness across my chest. I looked up at the ceiling, feeling my eyes begin to sting as my duty became clear.

"You don't have to come with me, John."

"Of course I do," I said almost fiercely. "Of course I do."

"Why?"

"Because…because I can't let you go alone. Because we've been tied up in chairs. Because you might be right."

The horizon disappeared.

"We have to go," I said, not looking at him. "We have to go and try to save the world."

"Or at least save someone."

We stood in that room together, trying to grasp the weight of the decision we were making. I did not know who I was anymore. I did not know what I was doing. All I knew was that everything I thought I knew seemed to be coming undone.

PART TWO

The Criminals

7

The limousine swung slowly around the parabolic driveway, and the gravel crunched beneath the tires. I bent down to look through the window, but I still could not see the top of the massive mansion. Even the word *mansion* does not do justice to the sheer, intimidating enormity of the structure.

The past day had been a whirling chaos. Hart had taken Grey and me to a hotel, and we had washed ourselves and been provided with a few fresh sets of clothes. Hart gave us back our wallets and most of the other personal effects we had carried with us when we were kidnapped.

Hart had told us that a certain level of formality would be required of us in the mansion and that we would have to do our best to operate within the bounds of high-society decorum. Neither Grey nor I were much accustomed to luxury, but we assured him we would do our best.

"What about you?" I asked. "Why aren't you being outfitted with suits and luggage?"

"My role is going to be less on the foreground. You two may not see much of me, but don't worry, I'll be keeping an eye on you."

"I'm glad to hear it."

I still did not trust Hart, and I did not think he trusted me. Grey seemed to trust him though, so I put my doubts aside at least for the moment.

Now Hart drove the limousine. He was outfitted with the ensemble of a chauffeur. As the car ground slowly to a halt and my mind slowed with it, I reflected for a moment on the enormity of our undertaking. But I only had a moment before the car had stopped completely. I was attired in clean and casual business wear: freshly pressed khaki pants, a crisp white shirt with a stiff collar, and a blue tie with a pleasingly symmetrical pattern. My shoes were shined, and my hair was combed.

I felt utterly unlike myself and only hoped that my discomfort was not obvious. I was now supposed to be a high-society iconoclast skimming through school on my father's money and accustomed to a life of luxurious leisure. I glanced at Grey. He hardly looked like the same person as the one I had seen on the rooftop of our prison. He was wearing a well-tailored dark suit with a shirt and tie. He had combed his hair before we left but rumpled it thoroughly during the drive. He did look as if he could be taken for an irresponsible highbrow. As he exited the limousine, he threw a sharp glance at his reflection in the tinted window and smiled briefly.

We crossed the rest of the drive and came to a stop before formidable wooden double doors, and then we gathered our courage like divers before a plunge. As I opened my mouth to speak, Grey reached out and pressed the doorbell definitively.

It was opened by an archetypal butler—small, frail, precise—who glowered at us with deep suspicion. I suppose every butler who knows his trade has mastered this slightly suspicious but impeccably polite expression.

I stepped forward with one foot and said, "Mr. Westfield and Mr. Grey for Dr. Monroe."

"Yes, sir. Right this way."

As we entered the house, I looked around me, expecting the massiveness of the house's exterior to have a corresponding atmosphere on the inside, decorated with the atrocities through which the members of the upper class have a penchant for displaying their wealth. The atmosphere of the house astounded me. It was so different from the wealthy homes I had observed as a child when I had been allowed to attend dinner parties with my parents.

The room we entered was certainly spacious but not with the sheer bulk of a house that attested to the affluence of its owners. Rather, the room gave the impression of having grown inside the house slowly and naturally. The house was elegant in its simplicity. It was full of curves and smooth lines. The furniture was purposefully placed, not elaborate. The settled beauty of the house intimidated and impressed me at once. Fuller's words about a subtle and complicated war came back to me. I realized that my guard was lowering already. It would take a great deal of resolve to be guarded in a place like this.

The butler led us into a circular foyer, which had a wide fountain in the center. I only saw a flash of doorways and staircases before we were led through one doorway on the right and up a winding staircase, through a sitting room, and through two open glass doors that led to a stretching balcony with a table laid only with a white tablecloth stretching from end to end.

A man stood with his back to us, his hands outstretched on the railing of the balcony, watching the staff setting up the garden for the forthcoming soirée.

"Dr. Monroe, a Mr. Westfield and Mr. Grey are here to see you."

The man turned around and smiled.

"Thank you, Edward."

As he turned around, I had a few moments to observe the man I had heard so much about. He was not a tall man, but his stance and demeanor communicated a youthful vigor and energy that made his presence daunting. He had dark hair, almost black, that stood out in waves from his head. The features of his face were precise, almost delicate. He had dark, arching eyebrows and deeply set, intense golden brown eyes. His mouth was small, curved into an easy, amicable smile. The sleeves of his white linen shirt were rolled almost to the elbow, and the top button of his collar was undone. He leaned back against the railing of the balcony, exuding confidence. He did not have the devilish, daring look I expected in a clever villain but did have disarming cheerfulness.

He surveyed us amusedly, as if he could sense our strained formality and desire to please him.

"What do you think of the place?" he asked sincerely, as if he but simply wanted to know.

"It's elegant," said Grey after a moment. "I admire the innovative architecture."

"You're welcome to look at the whole house and the grounds after you're settled in," he replied. "Your time is free until tonight. We'll be dining at 7:00 p.m. here on the balcony. Everyone will be here by then. You're two of the seconds, aren't you?"

"Yes," Grey said. "We haven't gotten our specific assignments yet, of course."

"Of course not," Monroe said with an unfathomable smile. He turned to watch a gardener trimming rosebushes below.

"You don't really know anything yet, naturally," he said, not turning around. "I'll explain it all tonight. You should be carefree right now. I'll give you the overview after the banquet, and your prime can explain the details of your component along the way."

"Of course," said Grey. "What rooms are we staying in?"

"Any room in the Quarter Wing. I'll have Edward show you."

Monroe walked back through the large glass doors and pressed a small button concealed by a green curtain that must be drawn over the doors at night. The butler appeared a few moments later.

"Edward," said Monroe, "show Mr. Westfield and Mr. Grey to the Quarter Wing and then have their luggage sent to their rooms."

"Yes, sir."

"Thank you, Dr. Monroe. We'll see you tonight," I ventured, trying to assert my presence. He rewarded me with a demure smile.

I followed Grey and Edward back into the house. We descended a different flight of stairs that went straight down into the foyer. Taking a closer look, I saw that the room curved into a circle, with marble floors and the majestic fountain in the center. The staircase we had descended was one of four that extended in different directions to a kind of indoor balcony that followed the rounded contour of the room. At the top of each staircase was an open doorway that appeared to lead to the different wings of the mansion. Across from the two middle staircases was the large set of wooden double doors that led to the mansion's entrance. I turned slowly around for a moment, forgetting my reserve and gaping at the breathtaking elegance of the place.

Edward and Grey were ahead of me now, proceeding to the staircase on the far left, which I deduced to be the Quarter Wing. I crossed the marble floor slowly, noticing the intricate design of the tiles. Every choice that went into the construction of this mansion consisted of the same grace.

We ascended the broad, carpeted staircase and through the doorway into the Quarter Wing. There must have been ten or fifteen rooms sprawling before us. Grey and I chose neighboring rooms, and Edward left us to give the orders about our luggage.

My room was consistent with the rest of the house: vast, tasteful, and elegant. The walls were ivory and the furniture something like mahogany. The room was decorated in subtle shades of green. I walked to the window and gazed down at the garden, which was comprised of a maze of pathways adorned with exotic flowers.

There was a quiet tap on the open door, and I turned to see Grey.

"Shall we explore?"

We wandered the Quarter Wing, examining the beautiful rooms. The heaviness in my heart lifted a little, and although the tight feeling in my chest never quite went away, a hopeful feeling began to flicker in me. I wondered if somehow we'd be able to accomplish our mission. No one was chasing us or trying to hurt us. Our lives were not in immediate danger, and we seemed also to have time—time to figure out what was happening and what to do.

We discovered that the Quarter Wing held a balcony, and from that balcony, a small set of stairs led up to a catwalk on the roof. Neither seemed to be in use, with only a round table and two chairs set on it. We climbed up to the catwalk, which ran the length of the roof with four small sets of steps, each descending to a balcony on different sides of the house.

We ventured back into the house and crept down the grand staircase into the foyer. I think we both felt a bit childish creeping around, half-afraid that someone was going to scold us for snooping, which made it all the more exciting. I wondered if all the members of the previous groups had done what we were doing.

We found our way into the kitchen. It had a bustling, familiar atmosphere that offset the rest of the house in its slapdash motion. The staff was hurrying around, and the cook was fussing at a delivery boy. Grey approached the cook and smiled at her.

"Are you getting ready for dinner tonight?"

The red-faced lady turned and looked Grey up and down, smiling a little and then frowning.

"I certainly am. The Banquet of Favorites is the most important event of the year."

"The what?"

The cook frowned at Grey and answered impatiently. "Everyone's favorite foods have to be on the table, and no room for mistakes!"

"I see," he said, giving her a winning smile. "And you've really managed to draw up a list of everyone's favorite meals?"

"Well, of course!"

She pulled a smudged list out of her apron pocket, and he reached for it, but she snatched it away.

"Now, I don't want you to go messing with the menu, young man. Dr. Monroe would have a fit."

"Oh, of course not," Grey assured her. "But may I just see it for a moment?"

She held it up for him to see, still gripping it tightly. Grey bent down to peer at it, then turned to me and smiled.

"Pot roast and macaroni and cheese?"

"What?"

"Under your name."

"That's incredible. How do you get this information?" I asked the cook.

"I don't," she said shortly. "Dr. Monroe sends me down the menu, and I find the right recipes for the items."

"The right recipes?"

A proud smile flitted across her face.

"That's right," she said. "We spend months researching recipes and taste-testing to prepare for the *Favorites*. Just you wait until dessert!"

I wondered if my favorite dessert would really appear before me tonight. Grey was wandering around the kitchen, looking curiously and intently at its contents, as if he were studying.

"What's your name?" he asked the cook.

"Mrs. Harrington."

"Mrs. Harrington, you have a lovely kitchen."

Mrs. Harrington nodded at him in grave appreciation.

"I doubt Monroe has ever been in his kitchen," I said as we walked out.

"I disagree," replied Grey. "He seems like the kind of man who takes a personal interest in how his house is run. When we met him this morning, he was watching the preparations of the banquet as if he had planned every detail and wanted to make sure it was all done right."

"Well, I hope for our sakes that you're wrong."

8

As Grey and I parted to dress for the evening, I could feel my nerves tingling with anticipation. Tonight would be the disclosure of the mission, the appearance of all the participants, and a chance to look more closely at the man behind it all. I stared at my open suitcase as all these thoughts passed through my mind. I put on the nicest clothes I had been given. Examining myself in the mirror, I thought I looked stiff and unnatural like someone in costume.

I emerged from my room and paced in the hallway for a few moments before Grey emerged, looking sharp and not as uncomfortable as I did. We descended the wide staircase back into the entry room with the fountain, and as I watched the patterns of light shining on the floor, I realized that the roof above us was made of glass that allowed the moonlight to stream through and reflect in the fountain.

It felt like a dream, as though the whole universe inside this mansion might be an illusion and shatter at any moment, giving way to the warm comfort of bed. In the dim light, the mansion seemed more sinister than when we had entered it a few hours before, and danger felt more immanent. Grey and I ascended the opposite staircase and found our way out onto the balcony. It was lit by strings of lanterns strung above our heads that made everything glimmer in shades of blue and violet. The table was spread with a black cloth, and all the dishes were silver. Grey and I searched for the settings with our names and found ourselves seated opposite each other.

No one else had come to the table yet, and I checked my watch to reassure myself that we had arrived promptly. We were a little early, and I waited impatiently for the clock to signal seven o'clock. Finally, I heard a distant chiming from somewhere inside the house, and as if they had been waiting for the cue, everyone came out onto the balcony before the clock had finished chiming.

It was an overwhelming moment, and I closed my eyes, breathing in deeply, willing myself to overcome the slight tremor in my upper body. I opened my eyes and looked straight ahead of me at Grey, whose eyes were roaming over the guests. There were a few moments of frantic confusion as chairs were pulled out, place cards examined, and seats switched. I had expected rigid silence, but there was the slight murmur of acquaintances greeting each other vaguely, as often happens before a business meeting. As the murmur dropped away, Monroe pushed back his seat at the end of the table and stood up. He wore a silver waistcoat over a black shirt with sleeves rolled up as they had been before. He smiled at everyone with the singular pleasure of a host about to begin a much-anticipated party.

"Good evening, friends," he said. Everyone's eyes were fixed on him, but no one spoke.

"Tonight, I invite you to join me in my annual Banquet of Favorites. It is a night for individual and intellectual pleasure, a night for indulgence in the very best of food and company. Do not hold back in your appetite or your opinions. Later on, we will gather in the garden for coffee and for our more serious discussion, but for now, you are simply to enjoy the finest things in life."

He sat back down and instantaneously a set of waiters appeared. They were dressed identically in black and white and each supporting a silver tray in his left hand with a black napkin draped over his right arm. They set the tray down in front of us and simultaneously lifted the lids. A strong panoply of aromas filled the air, and I smiled despite myself. There was my pot roast and macaroni and cheese. The roast came apart at the touch of my fork, and I took several rich, savory mouthfuls. The macaroni and cheese was almost unrecognizable with full, round noodles and a thick, creamy sauce topped with a layer of breadcrumbs. These truly were the finest things in life.

As I emerged from my bewitchment with the food, I became gradually aware of the conversations going on around me. I decided to take a slow and careful survey of the people around me one by one.

At the head of the table was Felix Monroe, looking confident and content. To his right was a man whom I guessed to be about my age. His head rose above the rest, and I knew that if he stood up, he would tower over the rest of us. Everything about him was long and thin; his face, arms, and hands all gave him the kind of endearing awkwardness of a boy in adolescence. He had glasses perched on his long nose and smiled as he listened to the diatribe of the woman across from him.

I examined this woman next. She was brown-haired and brown-eyed, talking rapidly about something that I could not hear. She was gesticulating wildly with her fork at the tall, thin man to reinforce her point. Occasionally, she would pause, out of breath, and he would respond with a word or two, only to have her laugh or shake her head and continue speaking, her eyes alight.

To the brown-haired woman's left and to my right sat a girl who had not spoken since dinner began. She had fair skin and dark red hair, and it struck me that I could not decide her age. Her face was freckled, which gave her a youthful air, but her quiet blue eyes gave her the look of wisdom, which implied experience. I caught all this from subtle sidelong glances, but I determined to speak with her later.

To my left and at the other head of the table sat a rather heavyset young man with fair hair who had not ceased speaking since dinner began. He spoke to Grey, who was across from me and to his left, and I discovered that his name was Peter Allen. Grey watched him, quiet and smiling, and asked him a series of questions he was more than happy to answer. His demeanor was comfortable and expansive, more like a host than a guest, and he had the good-natured clumsiness of someone who was eager to please by any means except the one most suited to his company.

The seat between Grey and the tall man was empty, and I wondered what kind of person would be absent from such a dinner. I chose this question as a good opening for my conversation with the girl to my right. I turned a little in my seat. The girl was gently stirring the steaming bowl of soup before her, and she looked at me inquisitively.

"Do you know who is supposed to be sitting across from you?" I asked.

"No," she said quietly, not with hostility, but simply in a disinterested way. She offered me nothing more and I turned, defeated, to take another bite of my meal. I tried again.

"What's your name?"

"Katherine Stewart."

"John Westfield."

She only nodded as if she had already known. I shifted in my seat. Finally, I produced another question.

"Do you know anyone here?"

She glanced around the table, scrutinizing.

"I know Felix Monroe, of course. And I know Peter Allen." She nodded at the animated young man speaking demonstratively to Grey. "And I know Claire Cunningham."

She tilted her head toward the brown-haired girl to her right and added, "I'm her second."

"I see," I said, although I did not. We relapsed into silence, and again I gazed around the table. I felt my left elbow jostled and looked over to see Peter Allen looking at me with round eyes.

"Why do you think Daisy isn't here?" he said in a low but still loud voice.

"Who?"

"Daisy Belton. She's supposed to be a prime, especially since there are only eight of us this year."

"I count seven."

"No, no, eight. Monroe is in the field this year."

"You mean he's—"

"Part of the mission, yes. I am sure he is going to be a prime. I wonder who gets to be his second."

"What about you?"

"I'm Stephen's second."

This must be the tall, thin man, I thought. I took in all the information. Peter Allen had gone back to chatting vigorously with Grey, and I sat silently for a few minutes, grateful for my stoic companion.

At last, everyone stood up from dinner and retired to their rooms. Grey and I walked up the stairs of the Quarter Wing in silence. We stood at the top of the stairs for a moment. Then without a word we parted.

When I came out of my room a few minutes later to wait for Grey, I saw that the door to his room was open and that the room was empty. Surprised and a little disgruntled, I walked down the stairs alone, wondering where the garden was. I ran into Edward, who looked at me in stately disapproval.

"How can I best get to the garden?" I asked in my most dignified manner.

"If you go through the doors beneath the Full Wing, you will find a path that leads you to the garden," Edward replied and walked away, not waiting for a response.

I looked up for a moment, located the stairs to the Full Wing, which I guessed was the rightmost, walked up the stairs, and found large wooden double doors. I opened them and found a series of paths leading in what seemed to be all different directions. I sighed and took a survey. Nearly straight ahead of me I could see the glow of more lanterns. I headed toward them, and the murmur of voices gradually illuminated my ears. I walked through an elaborate archway and found myself in a sort of arena hemmed by tall hedges, blooming with flowers, with lanterns strung on the trees. Wicker chairs were arranged in a half-circle, and a table not far away held cups and coffee pots. I walked over to it, and the man behind the table handed me a cup of coffee.

I splashed a little cream in my coffee and seated myself in one of the wicker chairs, looking around to see who had arrived. Grey was sitting in a chair on the farthest end of the semicircle, silent and stoic. I began to feel more isolated, wondering if I was going to be left to defend myself in the end.

The tall man sat in the middle of the semicircle, his long legs stretched in front of him and his hands folded behind his head. Peter Allen sat in the chair beside him, looking restive, chattering away, almost completely ignored by his companion. Katherine Stewart sat a little to my left, looking much the same as Grey but more perceptibly tense.

Grass crunched behind me. Claire Cunningham, with a quick step, approached a chair beside me and dropped into it, turning toward me impulsively.

"This is the exciting part, isn't it? Are you nervous?"

I nodded and shrugged.

"Don't worry," she said, looking at me thoughtfully. "You seem like the kind of person who picks up on things quickly. I don't think you'll have any trouble, and you're a second, aren't you?"

Her manner of stringing several thoughts together in a sentence was disarming, so I just nodded again.

"Remind me of your name," she demanded.

"Jack Westfield."

She smiled as if the name told her everything she needed to know.

The next person to speak was Felix Monroe himself, who strode into the garden and pulled a chair out in front of the rest. He sat down and looked slowly around the circle. I wondered what he thought of the missing conspirator.

"Comrades," Monroe began, "this year's scheme is a unique one. There will be more room for improvisation, more necessity of theatrical talent, and more dependence on unity than there has been before. There are only eight members, including myself. That means only four primes and, of course, four seconds. Don't worry," he said, smiling at Claire who was shifting a little in her seat. "Daisy will be here."

"It is important," he continued, "for us all to know each other. Your most important relationship is with your partner. Seconds, you must be familiar with the intricacies of your prime's assignment and also their methods. That way, if a transition is necessary, it will be smooth. Primes, do not underestimate the value of getting to know your seconds. There is a reason we are all in the same house together."

Monroe looked above our heads as if gathering and reviewing the various details of the plan in his mind, and then he looked back down at us and smiled.

"The scheme itself is simple. As always, there was no need to create conflict. Conflict came to us. Our target this year is a politician. He is running for governor of this very state, and his campaign has succeeded in making him popular. However, I have found a skeleton in his closet, begging to be released.

"Nineteen years ago, after our target, Mr. Brown, had been married for ten years, he had a series of embarrassing and nearly detrimental losses in court. His career was on the brink of failure, and his professional abilities and personal character were being seriously called into question. A few years later, he managed to recover, redeem himself, and is now more remembered for the recovery than the failure.

"However, unnoticed by most of his professional colleagues, many of his personal friends, and certainly the world in general, during the slump in his career, Brown disappeared for three months, ostensibly in a leave of absence. But almost no one knows where he went, not even his wife.

"I found out where he went. The actual location is unimportant. He was in a big city, living in a hotel, changing rooms every week, and most importantly, having a rather long and complicated relationship with a woman who was not his wife. When Brown returned from his disappearance, he was able to salvage and resume his career, and the details of his absence were left undiscovered and forgotten, until now."

Monroe paused and surveyed his audience, all silent.

"As I said, it has been nineteen years since his disappearance and affair, and now he is running for governor. Our scheme this year is simple. We are going to remind Mr. Brown that the past is never truly forgotten and bring him face-to-face with his ghosts."

"Exactly how are we going to do that?" asked the tall man.

"We are going to bring him his long-lost child."

Monroe nodded to the back row, and we all turned to see his object. When I saw it, I felt as if an anvil had been dropped on my chest. I simply sat and stared, knowing in that instant why I had been chosen for this mission and knowing irrefutably that there was now no turning back.

9

I felt sick, dizzy. I remember the questions and replies that evening only vaguely. I remember the feeling of the chair beneath me and the texture of the grass when I finally rose at the end of the night and walked back into the mansion. Somehow I found my way back to the Quarter Wing and up the staircase to the roof. I stood on the catwalk, looking out at the sky, which was chaotic with stars. They seemed unbearably bright, as if my eyes were suddenly too sensitive and the light was hurting me. I do not know how long I stood there before I heard Grey's voice behind me.

"Jack?"

I turned and looked at Grey. He looked unfamiliar, and I remembered what a stranger he really was. I felt confused and my head ached. I looked back at the sky, hoping he would go away again.

"Are you all right?"

His voice felt cold and distant, as if he were a long way away. I shook my head. He came closer, and I continued to stand motionless.

"After you saw Daisy Belton, you looked sick."

He observed this detail impartially. I looked at him again. He was so close that I could see his eyes.

"My parents died in a car accident."

"I'm sorry."

"The next year, my uncle and aunt sent my little sister and me to two different boarding schools. Six months later, the boarding school sent my aunt and uncle word that Danielle had gone missing. My aunt and uncle did not tell me about it until they had done everything they could. They told me not to worry, and I decided to stay where I was. Two years later, she was declared to be dead after a girl her age was found washed up on shore near her school. A boating accident, they said."

Grey nodded, not taking his eyes off me.

"I should have gone to look for her, of course, tried to find her. I never should have given up on her. I have made a few attempts over the years, but eventually I stopped. It has been eleven years since I last saw her, since our parents died. I saw her again tonight."

Grey was watching me in motionless surprise.

"She must have changed her name to Daisy Belton, always liked *The Great Gatsby*, but she is really Danielle Westfield. She is my sister. She is nineteen years old. I don't know how she…all these years…"

My broken sentences trailed off, and I was lost in thought. Then I turned and looked angrily at Grey.

"She never tried to contact me. She let me think she was dead. She ran away, and now she is part of a gang of conspirators that is going to blackmail a politician and dredge up his past for amusement. Why? How did she become involved with these people?"

"I don't know. You haven't seen her since she was nine. Are you sure it's her?"

I slammed my hands against the rail, and it made a hollow sound that disappeared into the air. A thousand thoughts were whirling in my mind. I thought about the day my parents died, about crawling into bed beside Danielle and stroking her hair. I thought about watching her, sitting forlornly on top of her suitcase in the back of our neighbors' car, being driven to boarding school. I looked at Grey, and he was watching me intently.

"At least now you know why you're here," he said.

"This isn't a reason to be here. This is how they are manipulating me to stay!" I said, my voice rising. "Well, it is *not* a reason to stay. It's a reason to take Danielle out of this place and never look back."

"She seems to want to be here."

"Well, we seem to want to be here too, but we don't."

"We chose to be here."

"After they held us hostage for three days."

"It is unlikely that there are any other double agents here but us," Grey said. "That means that your sister chose to be here like everyone else. She wanted to be chosen for this. Somehow, she found her way into high society and learned about Felix Monroe and applied or whatever it was to be chosen for his secret society. You aren't going to be able to drag her out of here unnoticed. Even if you did, what is the likelihood that you could escape without being caught and injured or killed? Monroe seems to know more about us than we know about ourselves. I highly doubt that he has *no* contingency plan for conspirators who change their minds and try to leave."

His speech had only made me angrier, and I moved away from him like a petulant child.

"She's going to know I'm not part of this society when she sees me," I said. "She'll blow our cover."

"Why? She has not seen you for eleven years. She has changed. Why couldn't you have?"

"I didn't change."

"You could have. That's all that matters."

"You want me to lie to her?"

"That may be the only way to save her. She needs to believe that you've changed—that for some reason you *want* to be here."

I closed my eyes, trying to fend off the nightmare. Without opening my eyes, I said to Grey, "You're her second, aren't you?"

"I am."

"I want you to tell me what she says. I want you to learn about why she is here. Then tell me everything you learn."

Grey did not speak for a few moments, then said in a quiet but unyielding voice, "Listen to me. We have come here on a mission. We are going to stop these people without getting caught, but only if we stay calm and work together. I will learn as much about Danielle as I can, but you are going to have to concentrate on your own tasks. There cannot be any foolish mistakes made from panic, or it will all be for nothing."

He stopped and looked at me. I put my hand to my head.

"It's a nightmare."

He nodded.

"Do you know exactly when the plan goes into action?"

"He didn't say," answered Grey. "I expect we'll learn more tomorrow."

"So what's our plan?"

"For now, to follow the protocol. Do whatever they tell us to do. We have a few days, I think. Maybe even a week."

"How are we going to get our information to Fuller?"

"Through Hart, I think."

"I don't trust him."

"I don't trust anyone."

We stood in silence and watched the sky. I stopped waiting for the world to fall back into place. Nothing was going to be made right again. Grey and I were alone, working for people who had kidnapped us to stop a group of conspirators from blackmail. My mind wandered to Mr. Brown.

"I wonder if Monroe really is the only person who knows about Brown's mistakes," I said aloud. "Do you think he ever told his wife?"

"People are unpredictable," Grey answered after a few moments. "We spend years getting to know our family and friends, only to be shocked and disappointed by their decisions. I wonder why we are so surprised when we hardly know ourselves. We make mistakes we never expected to make, even the most predictable of us harbor ideas that would shock our closest friends. We have only the slightest fears and inhibitions between our wildest dreams and reality. If for a moment those inhibitions lower, there is no knowing where our minds will take us."

I ingested this speech in silence.

That night I lay awake, torturing myself by trying to recall every memory I had of Danielle. I could recall happy and sad memories, repaint them in the finest shades with an unnatural clarity. I was disgruntled to realize how sharply I could summon thoughts I had made great efforts to abandon. I remembered teaching Danielle to tell time. I remember the first time she told me what time it was—2:30 p.m.—and the way she threw back her little blonde head and laughed triumphantly.

My head ached. I eventually passed into a fitful sleep. After I awoke and dressed, I wandered down the stairs and into the kitchen. Mrs. Hamilton bustled about in her red-faced manner, giving orders, and attending to several tasks at once. She glanced at me when I came through the door as if I were another tomato that needed to be sliced and said brusquely, "Can I help you Mr. Westfield?"

"I was just wondering…about breakfast?"

She turned and put her hand on her hip.

"Give me your order and I'll make it."

"What do you have on hand?"

She frowned at me.

"Ms. Cunningham asked for cold cereal and coffee. There's some of that on the table."

She pointed to a swinging door at the end of the kitchen, and I exited obediently. Claire Cunningham sat at a long wooden table squarely in the middle of one side. A newspaper was spread out before her, and she was holding her coffee cup absently. When I entered the room, she looked up and smiled.

"Good morning, Ms. Cunningham."

"Claire."

"Good morning, Claire."

"Good morning…"

"Jack."

Claire glanced down at her newspaper and back up at me.

"The world is a mess, Jack."

"Yes."

"It always has been. I think it always will be."

Not knowing whether it was too early in the morning for philosophical discussion, I simply nodded pensively and poured my cereal. The dishes were clean and simple. I marveled again at the simplistic taste of our host. Despite Monroe's unlimited wealth, there was hardly a hint of wanton extravagance in his mansion.

I rather enjoyed Claire's commentary on life, and I prodded her a little to continue speaking.

"What do you mean a mess? If you think it's the way it's always been and always will be, then isn't that the way it's meant to be?"

"Yes."

Claire had been eating a spoonful of cereal and tapped her spoon lightly on the side of the bowl.

"I mean, it's a mess. It's complicated and chaotic. There are a lot of things that seem wrong with it, but those are only the small fragments of a big picture. Things are going the way they will, and nothing's going to stop them, but there's a lot of collateral damage that's hard to understand."

"Is it all leading somewhere?"

She had finished her breakfast and rose as I spoke.

"We'll see," she said and flicked a smile at me before she left the room.

As I sat at the table finishing my meal, Edward entered and handed me a note that read:

Westfield—

Meet me in my study at 10:02 a.m. Hallway beneath the Half Wing.

F.G.M.

I finished my breakfast and left the table, wandering into the entrance room. I watched the fountain for a few moments. There was a symmetrical pattern on the bottom in shades of red and blue. I stood gazing at it for longer than I thought, for by the time I checked my watch, it was 9:59, and I hurriedly scanned around for the Half Entrance. I guessed that it was beneath the middle staircase, and I found behind the stairs a long hallway lined with two long rows of doors.

I felt frustrated and vulnerable, helplessly studying the doors and trying to find the one to Monroe's study.

Halfway down the hallway, I found that one of the doors was open, and I entered to see Monroe looking at me with an impenetrable expression.

"Good morning."

"Good morning, Dr. Monroe."

"Call me Felix," he said, but I noticed that he gave the command differently than Claire.

"This morning, we are going to give each of our comrades their assignments and get to know them."

I nodded.

"You are my second, Jack. You understand what that entails, of course."

I nodded a little less certainly. He seemed to be waiting for an answer.

"I will learn the details of your position so that if anything should happen to make you unable to take your part in the...er...operation, I can take over."

"Yes. Do you know what my job is?"

"No."

"Mastermind. It is my job to know and understand each of the people who are components of the operation. I optimize their talents and emphasize their strengths. I am aware of their weaknesses and fears. Today we are only getting introductions. We will have short interviews with each of the members and give them their packets of instructions. If something happens to me, you will be the only one with the ability to contact all the members and ensure the success of the operation. There are always moments of improvisation, and you must be ready for them. For now, you can observe. Have a seat."

10

The first member to enter was Stephen Witherspoon. From the familiar ease of his movements as he sat down across from Monroe's desk and extended his long legs, I gathered that there was a preexistent understanding between him and Monroe. Perhaps they had already been friends, or perhaps Stephen Witherspoon had participated in earlier schemes. He appeared to be a few years older than the rest of us and perhaps the only one not intimidated by Monroe.

"Good morning, Stephen," said Monroe.

"Good morning, Felix," said Witherspoon, the corner of his mouth twitching ironically.

Monroe slid a large envelope across the table.

"Here's your packet of information. Study it carefully."

"Will there be a test?"

"There was only so much detail I could put in it."

Witherspoon opened the envelope and briefly thumbed through the papers. As he did, Monroe continued.

"You are going to be the lawyer, Stephen."

"Practical, since I'm a lawyer."

"Yes and a new one aside from the Finch scandal. All the documents you need are in there. You can decide how to present on your own. There are some guidelines, but much of it will be left to your style."

"A wise choice."

Witherspoon's eyes were half closed behind his glasses, as if he were almost bored by the conversation and found Monroe's exposition unnecessary. Monroe leaned forward on his desk for a moment, then sat back in his chair, folding his arms across his chest.

"What brought you back here?" he asked a little sharply.

"Money."

Monroe shook his head and sighed. Witherspoon put his hands behind his head and stared at the ceiling.

"You know why I'm here."

"Tell me."

"I like the business."

There was a pause as Witherspoon contemplated the ceiling. He let out a long sigh. I guessed that he felt he was above the explanation, but it seemed to be part of the ritual. At last he went on.

"I'm interested in loopholes. They're the realist's way of disillusioning all the people who deceive themselves into thinking the world works a certain way. People think that loophole finders—lawyers, businessmen, and especially children—are the ones who are trying to escape the rules and manipulate the situation to get their way. But it's the people with the loopholes who see things for what they really are. They poke holes in people's façades until their walls come crashing down. That's our mission with Mr. Brown."

Monroe nodded, his eyes fixed on Witherspoon, who gazed back at him, eyes still half closed and lips half smiling.

"You'll be my right-hand man during this scheme."

"I know."

Monroe's mouth tightened for a moment, then he smiled.

"You can go, Stephen. I'll see you later."

Witherspoon slowly stood up, took his packet from his desk, and left the room. Monroe sat still for a moment, then he glanced at his watch. Without looking at me, he asked, "What do you think?"

"He's an interesting man," I said dully. Monroe spun slowly to look at me.

"They are all interesting," he said. "What do you think about his reasons for doing it?"

I looked at the armrest of my chair. There was a small crack in the leather.

"I suppose it's a sort of game to him," I said tentatively.

"Yes, a game," Monroe echoed, looking at his watch again.

"He's practicing. He's practicing law," I said.

We were silent until there was another knock at the door at 10:18. This time, it was the silent redhead I had sat beside at dinner last night. She came and sat very still in the chair across from the desk, occupying much less space in the room than Witherspoon.

"Good morning, Katherine."

"Good morning, Dr. Monroe."

"Felix."

There was a pause.

"You've just completed your master's degree in journalism, I believe."

"Yes."

"You're starting your first job at the *Evening Chronicle* in a month."

Katherine nodded but remained stoic. After a pause, he slid her packet across the table.

"You are Claire's second. It is still very important for you to learn the details of her part in the operation because you may end up helping her, even if you don't completely replace her. There are a lot of details involved, a lot of work behind the scenes. There will probably be some technical aspects that are unfamiliar to you. If you need further explanation, ask Claire or me."

Katherine only nodded, unaffected.

"Do you have any questions for me?"

"Not yet."

He glanced at me.

"Do you have any questions, Jack?"

This seemed to be part of my training, so I thought about the questions he had asked Witherspoon.

"Ah, yes," I said, looking at Katherine.

"As a journalist," I began, grasping for a question, "what do you feel your calling to be?"

"I'm not sure I have one."

"What I mean is do you have a specific set of rules for yourself when it comes to your occupation?"

"That was not your first question."

"Well, no."

"Do you want me to talk about my rules or my calling?"

"I—"

"Frankly, I don't see how either is relevant to the present purpose."

"But why are you here, exactly?" I blurted, ashamed at repeating Monroe's question and thrown off at the girl's abrupt yet impassive interruptions.

"I am here to be Claire Cunningham's second."

Her literalness seemed to be obdurate. I grew more flustered.

"But why?" I asked like a small child incapable of understanding the self-evident truths of life.

"I don't think it matters," she said. "The course of my life has brought me here, not necessarily for a particular purpose, but it serves as a conduit for the next stage of my life and career. The nuances are irrelevant. Is there any other information I need?"

"No," said Monroe, and without taking her leave, Katherine rose and left the room. After the doors closed behind her, I could not remember anything she said. Monroe looked at me.

"That was your first shot," he said simply.

"I missed."

"You'll improve."

I was tense, waiting for the next person to come in. I felt a little relieved when Claire Cunningham entered. Of all the criminals I had encountered so far, I was most comfortable with her. I hoped Monroe might allow me to question her and redeem my previous failure.

"Good morning, Claire."

"Yes, it is," she said, smiling first at Monroe, then at me.

"You're doing your internship at the *Waldenburgh Chronicle*, aren't you?" asked Monroe.

"Yes, I am."

Claire shifted forward a little in her chair.

"It's not exactly what I thought it would be, but I'm learning a lot. After all those years in school, I'm still getting people coffee, you know? But that's the way it goes. I'm lucky they're letting me publish little things. You've read some, I guess."

She volunteered all this in her rapid, confident manner.

"I did, indeed," said Monroe, smiling. "I was quite impressed."

"Thank you."

"As I explained to Katherine, there is going to be more technical work in your part of the operation than you may be used to."

"I can handle it. My experience as an intern has taught me more about technical aspects than I ever wanted to know."

"If you have any questions about the equipment, don't hesitate to ask me."

"I won't."

"When I read your article about the Calloway crisis," Monroe began, and we had segued into the interrogation part of the meeting, "you seemed to be very confident that the events had a purpose and were not just the result of chaos or random violence, an unconventional point of view on the controversy."

Claire nodded.

"If they had a purpose, what do you think it was?"

"I don't know," said Claire, smiling as if the question were preposterous. Monroe raised his eyebrow.

"Yet you are confident in their significance?"

"I'm not."

Claire readjusted her position in the chair and stared at a spot on the wall for a few moments, her brow contracting.

"I think those things were going to happen, and there wasn't anything anyone could do to stop them," she said, her eyes steady.

"Then what do you think of the people who did them?"

"I think those people were wrong. I think the things we do, or try to do, define us, but I don't think we can change the way things are going to turn out."

"So as a journalist, what do you feel your calling to be?" asked Monroe without glancing at me.

"Telling stories."

"Elaborate."

"I find out what happens, identify what is most important about it, and tell it to the world so that they can feel informed, perhaps even feel as if they understand."

He nodded and the interview was over. The difference between the seconds and the primes was becoming clear. I began to understand why Monroe chose the way he did.

Monroe glanced at his watch and scowled.

"Peter Allen was supposed to be here three minutes ago," he told me without looking at me.

"Do you want me to go look for him?"

"We'll wait."

We waited for another two minutes before Peter Allen entered the room. He was red in the face and breathing hard.

"Everything in this house is hard to find," he said.

"Not if you know where to look for it."

"So," Allen huffed, plopping down in the chair, "do I get instructions today? How does this work?"

Monroe slid a packet across the table, and Allen unceremoniously opened it and began rifling through the contents, dropping and confusing the papers chaotically.

"Be careful with that," Monroe said acerbically. "Those contents should only be seen by you, Stephen, me, and if absolutely necessary, Mr. Westfield."

Allen nodded but continued flipping through the contents as if Monroe had said nothing. He looked up abruptly as Monroe began speaking.

"You are going to be Stephen's second. Hopefully, you won't have to do anything at all, but you should carefully learn the details of the plan in case you do."

Allen nodded.

"Mr. Allen—" Monroe began but stopped. He turned to me and asked, deviously I thought, "Mr. Westfield, do you have any questions for Mr. Allen?"

"Pete."

I thrashed about for a generic inquiry and at last landed on, "What do you think is our purpose as human beings?"

"To be happy," he answered without hesitation.

"Yes, well—"

"No, really," he interrupted earnestly. "I want to be happy. I think that's all anyone can do. All my decisions have been devoted to that belief."

"The belief that you were intended for happiness?"

He laughed loudly.

"I don't believe we were *intended* for anything. I think we live and then we die. And I think people waste a lot of time trying to find a purpose and a meaning in living when they could be being happy."

His abrasive words shocked me, and I cast about for a sequential question until I asked the one that came to mind.

"So why are you here?"

"It's good practicing—for being a lawyer, you know. And I think it's interesting. It will be great fun."

"You're not personally invested in it in any way?"

"I'm not personally invested in anything."

With those words, he rose, nodded to both of us, and exited the room.

In my head, I ran through the list of people we had interviewed so far and realized just as she walked in that it was likely I would see Danielle next. My throat tightened and a burning tingle surged through my chest. My heartbeat pounded in my temples, and I hoped violently that Monroe would not turn and look at me through the course of the interview.

"Good morning, Daisy."

"Good morning, Felix."

Danielle's appearance had vastly changed, but I could still trace a resemblance to the sister I had known eleven years ago. Her light hair was thick and long as always but now neatly arranged. She still had fair skin and a tendency to freckle. Her large brown eyes were the most alike in form but the most altered in expression. I remembered them as unshakably confident, warm, pure. Now they were cunning and sultry, eyes that had seen the world and viewed it with distrust and suspicion. It gave me a pang to look at them.

Danielle and Monroe talked while I made these observations, but I did not hear their words. He had explained her mission, but I had missed it. I would have to figure it out from what he said to Grey. She had not glanced my way when she entered the room, and I wondered if she had noticed me at all. When her eyes did fall on me, I saw her give a slight start. Her face grew a little pale, and her mouth opened a little, but she did not speak. She looked abruptly back at Monroe.

"Tell me why this scheme interests you, Daisy," he was saying. She gave a rather forced smile, I thought, and said vaguely, "It's quite a challenge...for an actress. It's the kind of reality, the kind of integrated experience that comes along only once in a lifetime."

Monroe did not seem impressed with her answer, but he nodded slowly.

"Yes, it is. And what do you think of the mission itself?"

"I believe in it completely," she said with sincerity that had not been present before. She leaned forward in her chair.

"Mr. Brown should be forced to face the consequences of his actions, and he never has been. People are not made uncomfortable often enough. If something shameful or dreadful happens, they pretend it didn't and move on with their lives. There are times, of course, when there's nothing else to be done. But if you are the perpetrator, you must know what you're doing, and if you don't, you ought to be reminded."

"Thank you, Daisy. You may go."

Grey was the last to come in. He did not look at me, but I was sure he knew I was there.

"Good morning, Mr. Grey."

Grey smiled and sat down.

"Mr. Grey, you are Ms. Belton's second. Have you been introduced yet?"

"No."

"Ms. Belton's function in the scheme is the most important of all. It is, above all else, an exercise in acting. She is going to be playing the role of Mr. Brown's long lost child. This involves a unity of emotion, conviction, and authenticity. She must be fully invested or it will not work. Of course, if all goes well with Ms. Belton, you will not have to do anything at all, but it is more important for you than any of the other seconds to be prepared to play, as there are other reasons you may become active. Do you understand?"

"Yes."

Monroe slid his packet across the desk, and he picked it up but did not look inside it.

"That is all your information about your role. Memorize it. The details must be so firmly in your mind that they would not escape you, even if you were put under a great deal of pressure."

Grey nodded and even smiled a little. He always smiled enigmatically, I thought, and I was not sure I liked it. Monroe seemed to feel the same way.

"Mr. Grey," he began, "in your academic endeavors, you have been pursuing psychology. I have chosen you as a second for Ms. Belton because I think your studies have given you a unique kind of insight into human nature and thus into some of the more subtle details of what this long-lost child might feel, what might drive the child to make contact with the father after nineteen years of existence."

"I feel confident that I can bring insight to that question."

The two men held each other's gaze for a long moment. At last, Monroe nodded. Grey exited silently, and the last of the interviews was over.

11

After the interviews were over, Monroe left his study without a word. I followed him, but he seemed to have forgotten me. He strode down the passage of doors and disappeared behind the Full Wing. I watched him go and paused in the front entrance, feeling lost and overwhelmed. I had expected to receive more instruction, and I wondered if I was supposed to know what to do. I had not been given a packet, so I could only suppose that Monroe intended to train me himself.

I resolved to look for Danielle. I decided to look in the garden. I walked outside and saw Witherspoon striding around the side of the house toward me. I tried to turn hastily aside, but he called my name.

"Westfield," he repeated, approaching with a piece of paper in his hand, "I need you to do me a favor."

I lifted the corners of my mouth in a polite smile.

"Of course," I said. "What do you need?"

He handed me two pieces of paper.

"I need you to pick up an order in town. Give them the name of Witherspoon and tell them that you need the Edford Division. Don't forget to tell them that or they won't give you the package. Give the address to the chauffer and the order slip to the proprietor of the shop."

"Right."

Witherspoon seemed to be the kind of man who, if he thought he could trust someone, did not bother much about it but let his mind wander to more important preoccupations. As I responded to his request, he was already looking over my shoulder at something else. Without concluding the conversation, he strode away, leaving me with a cryptic set of orders.

I stared at the order slip, wondering if I was supposed to understand what it meant. This might be a good chance for Grey and me to get away from the mansion. I walked into the house, glancing around for Edward. He emerged from one of the lower rooms with an ornate vase in his hands.

"Edward, have you seen Mr. Grey?" I asked in a commanding voice. He turned to me with superior disapproval.

"I think Mr. Grey is in the library."

"Where is the library?"

"Beneath the Three Quarter Wing, sir."

I had not been beneath the third wing before, but I found the enormous library without any trouble. The room had a high ceiling, and the walls were lined with large, simple bookcases. There were several bookcases in the middle of the room that formed something like private cubbies, inside of which were chairs or desks and lamps. It was an ideal arrangement.

I found Grey in a corner of one of these cubbies, sitting in a chair reading with his long legs stretched before him.

"Grey," I said, "do you have an assignment for this afternoon?"

"No…" he said abstractedly, glancing from me back to his book.

"I want you to come with me into town on an errand."

"What's the errand?"

I held up my slips of paper.

"I'm picking up a package for Witherspoon."

"What kind of package?"

"I don't know."

"But you're picking it up?"

"Yes."

He looked at me a little derisively but began to stand up. He glanced back down at his book.

"How are we getting there?"

"The chauffer is supposed to take us."

"Unfortunate."

We walked out into the foyer.

"How do we get the chauffer exactly?" Grey asked.

I cast about for inspiration.

"Ask Edward," boomed a voice from behind us as Peter Allen lumbered up.

"Just ask Edward to call a chauffer, and you'll be on your way before two minutes are up."

Allen called for Edward and requested the car. I hoped and prayed that he was not planning to accompany us. He talked incessantly until the car came, and I detected a disengaged look in Grey's eyes as he continued to nod and smile fixedly. I was relieved when the car came.

"I'd go. I'm up for a drive, but I've got a meeting with Witherspoon to ask him about some stylistic stuff. Of course, if I go into the field, I'm sure I'll do it differently than he would. In fact, I think I've got a pretty good idea of how it should be done, but Stephen's pretty set in his ways and doesn't take suggestions."

I nodded at him, and Grey and I stepped out the door.

"That man is exhausting," he said factually.

We slid into the car, and I slipped the address through the front seat to the driver. The car pulled smoothly away, curving around the driveway and out onto the road. We sat silently for a few minutes, then I began to broach the subject that I thought must be consuming us both.

"What do you think of the mission?"

Grey looked out the window, leaning his elbow on it and slipping his fingers beneath the hair on his temple.

"It is an interesting one. The idea is so simple. The question is: what draws each of the conspirators to commit to it?"

"I have some idea," I said. "They are a strange lot. They are so unrestricted by the restraints of ordinary people that they can be as idealistic and fantastic as they want without being undermined by reality."

Grey nodded, still thinking.

"Have you talked to my sister about her part in the operation?" I asked, trying to keep notes of anxiety out of my voice.

"Yes," he said. "After our interviews were over, Daisy and I went for a walk in the garden and talked about our roles."

"It's Danielle," I corrected.

"Not now," he said, looking at me seriously. "You must not call her, or think of her as, Danielle, or you might give yourself and her away."

"Has she told you how she got here?"

"Not yet. I think she will soon. She's made slight references to it, so I don't think she's going to be very hard to crack, but so far our relationship hasn't progressed to the informal. Thanks to Monroe's encouraging us to get to know each other, I don't think she'll mind very much if I ask her about her journey here, but I think it's better if she volunteers it on her own."

"How are you going to get her to volunteer it?"

Grey smiled.

"People like to talk about themselves, John. They like to talk about their lives and their thoughts and feelings. The more quiet or conceited ones tend to talk more about their opinions and ideas, but most everyone, if you take an interest in them and remember things about them, will eventually volunteer more for the sake of being understood."

"Interesting analysis. Whatever the case, I hope you can learn what brought her here so that I can figure out how to undo it."

"You think it can be undone?" he asked.

"You don't?"

"Not all things can be undone, Jack."

"This can. I can bring her back."

"This case is especially difficult because in order to bring her back, you would have to put yourself in danger and probably jeopardize our mission."

"But if our mission works, we will be able to rescue her anyway," I said fiercely. His glance shot toward me.

"Rescue her? Rescue her from what? She chose this, John. Whether or not she was led to it or convinced by it or believed in it, she came here of her own volition. Haven't you heard enough about this society to know that no one is in it by accident? Far from being coerced into it, people hear about it and want to be part of it but can't. It's only the unique, intense, radical people that Monroe chooses to be part of his group."

"He chose us."

"Yes, and haven't you wondered why?"

"Well, because of Danielle—"

"Monroe doesn't know she's your sister," Grey interrupted impatiently. "Monroe thinks that she is Daisy Belton because she has been for years. I think Monroe chose us because we are unique. We are outsiders, so focused and devoted to our interests that we exclude parts of real life that are natural to everyone else. We are ideal for an esoteric mission like this based on an abstract set of ideals that most people aren't dedicated enough to enact."

His words came to me through a fog. I could not understand how he could make such a judgment. How could he know what kind of life I had lived before Fuller's men had put a sack over my head?

"So you think Danielle is that kind of person too?" I said, ignoring his analysis of himself and me. "You think she is dedicated to a radical set of ideals like that?"

"I do," Grey said. "I don't think she's the same as you and I. I think her ideals are different, but as you may have noticed, a lot of different kinds of people are led to this mission."

"Right," I said. "*Led*. And I think we can lead her away."

"How?"

"I don't know yet."

We sat again in silence, looking out our separate windows, absorbed in our disturbing thoughts.

The car pulled up outside a dilapidated stone building that had a sign over it reading, "Anderson Arms." The building was sinister and did not even seem to be functional, but Grey and I walked up the stone steps to the wooden door and went in. The building was dimly lit by low lamps hanging from the ceiling and smelled like cigar smoke, the source of which was a small huddle of men sitting by a fireplace at the end of the room. The rest of the room was filled with booths, about half of them occupied by people eating. The clink of sturdy dishes and the murmur of voices mingled with the smoke, and my eyes wandered until I saw a high wooden counter a little offset from the center of the room.

We walked up to it, and a frail grey-haired man leaned his elbows over the counter and looked at us.

"How can I help you?" he asked.

Dreading that my words would be meaningless to him, I said stiffly, "I've come to pick up an order for Mr. Witherspoon. The Edford Division."

He raised his eyebrows.

"Ahh, yes," he said. "Wait right here."

He trotted to a door in the corner of the room and disappeared. Grey and I waited uncomfortably, looking around the room and watching the people.

As we stood there, waiting for a mysterious package that, for all we knew, might have been a bomb or a hole in the head, a thought occurred to me: we were out of the elegant prison that had been trapping us until now. In fact, this was the first time since I had been knocked unconscious that I was not in a prison of some sort. I glanced around the room.

"Grey—" I said under my breath.

"John." He said my name sharply, as if to stop what I was going to say next.

"What?" I asked.

"….expect the mission to go off without a hitch, don't you?"

I looked at him out of the corner of my eye. What was he doing?

"Which…"

"Mr. Brown, you know. It's going to be flawless."

Why wasn't he letting me speak?

Then I saw it. It was just a movement in my peripheral vision. There was a man sitting in the corner of the dark room cradling a mug of something hot between his hands. He was not watching us—not even looking at us. Yet, when I glanced his way, I felt a chill run down my spine—the kind of chill you get when you know for certain that you're alone, yet some part of you feels as if you're being watched.

The grey-haired man appeared again with a younger man behind him carrying a large package, which he handed to me.

"Tell Mr. Witherspoon thank you for the business," he said with a smile. I nodded and Grey and I left as quickly as we could. With my elbow, I tapped the front window of the car waiting outside. It rolled down, and I saw that it was Hart who had been our chauffer this whole time.

"Can you open the back?" I asked through the window. He leaned down and pressed a button, and I deposited my package.

"What is it?" he asked.

"I really don't know," I said. We all got back in the car and it pulled away quickly.

"It's a little unnerving to think that we don't know what we're carrying around," Grey said.

"True, but it's doubtful that the objects are harmful in and of themselves. From listening to the interviews, I suspect it's surveillance equipment."

"From *that* place?"

I shrugged.

I glanced out the window and realized that we were not headed back to the mansion.

"Who was that man in there?"

"Monroe."

"What?" I sat up straight and whipped away from the window to look at Grey. "How could it possibly have been Monroe?"

"I'm fairly certain I know what happened."

"Please disclose your insight, then."

"Monroe had Witherspoon send you on an errand—to see if you would bring me, to see if you would go, to see where you would go next. He knows we're not going back to the mansion right now."

"We're—"

I skimmed the unfamiliar territory outside the window.

"Where are you taking us, Hart?" I asked.

In answer, he pulled up in front of a building and parked the car. The building was large, square, and gray. It looked even more uninviting and unimportant than the last.

"Get out."

Grey and I slowly stepped out of the car.

"What are we doing here?" I asked.

"Follow me."

Feeling anxious, I mounted the steps after Hart and Grey, and the three of us entered a small side door. We walked down a narrow hallway, turned and walked down another exactly like it until we approached a large set of double doors. It was not until I heard the heavy metallic slam of the doors closing behind us that I realized at last where we were.

12

Hart had brought us to the building where Grey and I had been held captive at the beginning of our journey. Previously, we were blindfolded going to and from it, but now we could observe everything about it. There was not much to observe; it was grey, dingy, solemn, and bare. From the outside, it appeared to be an abandoned factory or workshop, most likely empty and unused.

Hart led us down a corridor and then another, both of which resembled each other. We entered a room that I recognized as Fuller's office, and this time, I felt more comfort than intimidation entering it.

Fuller was sitting in his chair behind his desk and rose as we entered, motioning us to three chairs in front of his desk. Hart, Grey, and I all sat down. Fuller sat and surveyed us in silence. His fingertips were pressed together, his elbows resting on the arms of his office chair. He looked intently at each of us for what felt like a long time, and finally he spoke.

"Do you have an assessment for me?"

He looked at me, so I spoke first.

"Right now, we are only beginning to figure out what the mission is," I said blankly. "I don't think we have much helpful information for you."

During the following silence, I began to think hard about what kind of information I had and what I should tell Fuller. I had heard something valuable from each of the individual conspirators and assimilated Monroe's instructions to them to form a faintly visible idea of the operation's design. If I gave Fuller all the details, he would not have enough details to put an end to the scheme but enough to make a blunt and imprecise blow to prevent it. I wanted more time to figure it out, to find out why my sister was there and if I could remove her from being caught up in the middle of a feud between two groups, neither of which seemed to be in possession of a full set of ethics.

Fuller turned to Grey.

"What do you think of these people?"

"They're very interesting—" began Grey.

"We don't have a lot of details," I interrupted. He looked at me curiously. Fuller looked from one of us to another.

"True," Grey affirmed quietly. "I think we need more time to gather details before we can give you a full picture of the operation."

Hart looked at me.

"Weren't you part of some kind of interview of each of the members, Westfield?"

"Yes, but that was more, you know, to get to know them, to indulge the whim of Monroe. There wasn't a lot of talk about the details."

Hart scowled and I looked down at my hands. I wondered if Fuller guessed about my divided loyalties.

"Next time," Fuller said quietly, "I'll need more information."

We rose and began to leave.

"Wait a minute, Mr. Westfield."

Hart ushered Grey out the door, and I turned to look at Fuller. His eyes were fixed on me, and I felt my features stiffen, resisting.

Fuller stood and came close to me. We were face to face. We were about the same height; I may even have been a little taller.

"Jack," he said quietly and steadily, "I chose you for this mission for a reason."

"I know," I said, desperate frustration rising in my chest. He looked at me again.

"It's not an easy task. Make sure that your personal investment is a help and not a hindrance. Use it as an advantage. You are doing the right thing, even if it is painful."

I nodded but said nothing.

"Jack," he added, as if he had just resolved in his mind to say what came next. "There's something else I think you ought to know about Grey."

I watched Fuller's face and felt that many decisions were being made behind it.

"His past is…less than stellar."

"What do you mean?"

"When we—found him—he was participating in some legally questionable acts."

"What kind of—"

"The nature of the acts is not important," Fuller interrupted, "I just thought I might warn you that temptation—doubt, questioning—might be more of a problem for Grey than it is for you."

"I see."

"Just watch him, will you?"

"I will."

Fuller gave me a dismissing nod, and I walked quickly down the corridor after Hart and Grey. We got back into the car and began driving back to the mansion. Neither Grey nor I spoke a word, but I could feel him watching me as I looked out the window.

Edward greeted us at the door of the mansion and told us that there would be an assembly in the garden at 6:00 p.m. Grey and I separated and went to our rooms. I lay on my bed, staring at the ceiling, trying to work up a plan to save us all from this mess. I knew that stopping Monroe and defeating his scheme was Fuller's mission, but I was more occupied with saving my sister than saving the world. I envied Grey's detachment and ability to analyze the situation without any personal investment.

At 6:00 p.m., I walked to the garden and sat in the same chair as I had the first night, watching everyone assemble in the same manner they had before. I looked around for Grey and saw him solemnly sitting beside

Danielle. A familiar mixture of fear and frustration welled up in me. She was so familiar and so untouchable.

I will not recount the exact details of our meeting that night. Felix Monroe told us that the next day, we would all go to *L'Hôtel des Rêves*, an extravagant hotel about half an hour's drive away. There were rooms reserved for us, each prime and second would be together, and the next morning at 11:00 a.m., the operation would launch. The reality of it, saturated by the details of the scheme, began to weigh heavily on me, and I found that by the end of Monroe's detailed instructions, my breath was labored and heavy.

No one except for Peter Allen spoke a word, and we all retired back to our rooms. Before I had reached the Quarter Wing, Monroe caught up with me and handed me not a packet but a long, thin metal box. He looked at me with grave confidence.

"These are the details of the scheme, Westfield," he said. I looked down at the box, trying to disguise my apprehension and my shaking hand. Monroe put his hand on my shoulder. "Everything you would need to run the scheme without me is in this box. Do not open it unless it is absolutely necessary."

I noticed that the lock on the sheath was engraved with the initials *L.G.* It seemed strange that his lock did not bear his own initials. It seemed strange too that he had not yet given me the combination for the lock. I had already been given my second's packet and I could not imagine what further objects or information this mysterious box might contain. Whatever it was, it seemed to be even more sensitive and valuable than what I had received at the beginning. I half expected it to explode at any moment. It was about the same size and shape as whatever it was we had retrieved for Monroe on our outing.

"Keep the box with you at all times, but open it *only* if something happens to me and I am unable to complete the operation."

"Are you worried that something is going to happen to you?"

He smiled wryly.

"I don't expect anything to happen to me, but there is almost always some complication or other. We have had to use seconds several times, and occasionally one of our primes has been put into physical danger."

I nodded, not knowing what to say. With a firm tap on my shoulder, Monroe said once more, "Only open if it is necessary. That is information no one except for me is supposed to have. Hopefully, you will not have to use it."

"What is the combination?"

"I'll tell you tomorrow."

Back in my room, I put the box on my desk and stared at it. There were several options of what I could do with it. I could open it, of course, and use it to try to stop the mission myself. I could take it directly to Fuller and let him decide what to do with it. It was very unlikely that I would be able to use it to blackmail Monroe myself since he probably covered his own tracks far too well to hand over incriminating evidence to anyone. If I opened it, he would know soon.

Perhaps an hour had passed in consideration of these options when I heard a knock at my door. I jumped up and childishly hid the packet beneath my bed, somehow not wanting anyone to know I had it, and opened my door to find Hart confronting me.

"We are going to the hotel tomorrow," he said obviously.

I nodded and opened my door a little wider, allowing him to come in. We stood awkwardly in the middle of the room.

"This is probably your last chance to take a message to Fuller."

"I can't leave the mansion unnoticed now."

"I can take a message or any kind of information to Fuller for you."

I wondered if he had somehow seen Monroe give me the box. I was not at all sure that I was ready to hand it over yet.

"I don't know anything new," I said half-truthfully. Hart simply stood gazing at me.

"Hart, how did you come to work for Fuller?" I asked, surprised at my own bluntness.

"Fuller is in the business of righting wrongs," he answered. "I believe in what he does."

"And yet from what I can tell, he doesn't seem particularly concerned with the dictates of the law," I pointed out. Hart smiled.

"The law is not in the business of righting wrongs," he said.

"Then what is it in the business of?"

"Of setting up a system intended to prevent wrongs from occurring, and once they have occurred, in punishing the perpetrators of those wrongs."

"It sounds like the same thing."

"It's not the same thing, Westfield. The law is not always effective. It cannot repair the damages done. It can't avenge them. It does not discern between differences in motive and situation. It is blind. Fuller is not blind. He sees and discerns. He sees what the blind law cannot, but he is powerless to take it on by himself. That's where I come in."

We stood silently for a few moments before I finally decided to risk another question.

"How did you find him?"

"He found me."

Hart began to leave. At the door, he turned.

"The law is not everything, Westfield."

He was gone. I stood and sat and paced for hours as the world outside my window grew dark. At last I wandered up to the catwalk.

I thought I might find Grey there, and I was right.

Something had happened to me the moment I was knocked unconscious, and I think something had happened to him too. Life had changed. Darkness had closed in on me for the first time in a long time. Darkness is terrifying in its formlessness. Evil is covered by the dark; sin goes unseen, crimes go unpunished, and the distinction between good and evil becomes difficult to distinguish. Darkness makes deeds permissible to those who will shrink from them at dawn.

I saw Grey's frail figure etched against the dim gleam of the moon. For a moment, I froze, my heart pounding, coldly certain that he was about to slip gently off the edge of the building—the edge of the world—and escape the darkness forever. I shivered.

Grey turned and looked at me. Among the confusion of the past days, among all the people I had met, Grey remained in my mind as the only one I could trust. With a curious sense of calm, I walked toward him and saw that he was holding something. It was a beautiful ornament, glimmering in its frail geometry. I had seen it poised gracefully somewhere in the mansion.

"I'm going to drop it," he murmured quietly as if to himself.

"Why?"

The wind blew toward us, and he breathed it in as if he needed it inside of him.

"Because it's so beautiful.

Another breeze, another breath.

"I don't have to throw it," he continued. "I only have to let go, and the world itself will pull it and drag it down—*down*—until it hits the pavement."

His speech began to come faster.

"And when it hits the pavement, it will smash. It will shatter into a thousand tiny fragments. Then everything will be still again, and the ornament will lie there, only it won't be an ornament anymore. It won't be anything anymore. It will just be broken glass."

"Grey—"

"Once I let go, it can never be undone."

He looked at me, a strange light in his eyes.

I felt fury swelling in me like a storm. I was angry with Grey and his calm despair. He stood erect, looking at the ornament in his hand. We stood for a long time. A drop of rain hit my shoulder, and I looked up to see clouds moving toward the still moon. I heard the small, clear sound of the raindrops hitting the ornament. The rain grew faster with uncharacteristic rapidity. Grey began breathing more quickly. I saw his hand tremble for a moment.

There are few instances when two things truly happen at once, but this was one of them. I flung myself at Grey, and with a barely perceptible motion, he let the ornament go. We both hit the ground at the same moment I heard the ornament shatter. My rage broke open, and for a few moments, I blindly fought him, swinging and thrashing wildly and bitterly, relishing the pain of his ripostes. Rain was in my eyes. I felt hot and breathless.

After what felt like a long struggle, but in reality was probably the work of a few moments, we collapsed side by side against the railing of the roof, both breathing heavily.

At last, I asked the question that had been bothering me since the day I met him.

"What's your name?" I shouted violently over the wind and rain. "Your real name?"

He gave me an indescribable look.

"It's Lawrence," he said. "Lawrence Grey."

As if the pronouncement of his Christian name had broken a dam within him, Grey let out a groan and began to speak.

"I've lived alone all my life, Jack."

I nodded. "So have I."

"My mother died a few years ago. I never knew my father."

I gazed at him silently, no words presenting themselves as an appropriate response.

"I've stolen—I've cheated—I've done nearly everything but kill."

Something did a turn within the walls of my stomach.

"I've got nothing to lose."

The rain continued to tap on our shoulders, our faces, arms, and legs, but we sat still, accepting it.

"Mr. Brown—do you think he deserves this?"

"What do you mean?"

"Do you think he deserves to be confronted?"

"I think," I said slowly, "that if Danielle really were his long lost child, there would be nothing wrong with her trying to find him—to ask him for answers. But she isn't, Grey," I said, hearing the defeat in my own voice, "Justice isn't ours to give."

13

All members of the group assembled at breakfast the next day. I watched Grey carefully. He ate with precision and very little. There was the hint of the small gash I had made on his face the night before. I felt the bruise around my eye. Grey's face was pale.

Peter Allen talked noisily. Monroe and Witherspoon conversed quietly and rapidly at the end of the table. Katherine Stewart sat silently. Danielle sat next to Grey, and they occasionally exchanged a few words. Claire Cunningham sat beside me and eventually spoke.

"Are you nervous?" she asked.

"Not really."

We ate the rest of our breakfast in silence.

We divided up into two cars and drove to the hotel. Everyone was paired except for Monroe and me.

Monroe, desiring his own room, had reserved separate but adjoining rooms for the two of us.

Walking into *L'Hôtel des rêves* was a strange experience. Everything was foreign with a blinding sense of luxury. There were vast arching ceilings and pillars that seemed to have grown into them. The details were lost in a blur of light and color. I was sent up to my room after a few moments, and I surveyed my new surroundings. I had been instructed to arrive at Monroe's door at 10:40 a.m. to prepare for the conference with Mr. Brown at 11:00.

The day was long and I spent most of it alone. As the night began its laborious passage, I paced my room, worrying about Danielle and the operation and trying to determine what I ought to do. I wondered if Fuller was going to intervene, if Hart had realized or communicated where we were going. If I moved too soon, Monroe would shut the whole mission down and withdraw without a trace. But any move I could make from here on out seemed almost too late.

Shortly after 3:00 a.m., there was a quiet knock on my door.

"Who is it?" I asked.

"Lawrence Grey."

I opened the door. There he stood, looking almost as disheveled as I but less distraught. His face was haggard but calm.

"Jack," he said and then hesitated. I looked at him inquisitively.

"I want you to go about the operation tomorrow just as planned."

"What?"

"Don't do anything to interfere, just do your job exactly as—"

"What's your plan?"

"It is better if you don't know."

"I'm supposed to be your partner."

"Then trust me."

I looked him in the eye and saw that he was calm and confident. I was at a loss. After a few silent seconds, Grey turned to go. He turned back momentarily at the door and said, "She's going to be all right."

I nodded. A flicker of a smile crossed his face.

"Good night, Jack."

"Good night, Lawrence."

The next day, I arrived at Monroe's door promptly at 10:40 a.m. Everything happened quickly.

"Here's the plan," Monroe said. "Cunningham is in the conference room now, setting up some of the equipment we will need to retrieve later on. Witherspoon will be waiting in the conference room at 11:00 a.m. to present Mr. Brown with the choice of lawsuit and scandal or a confrontation with his long lost child. He will, of course, choose the child. At precisely 11:30, Belton will enter and play the heartbroken child. All the seconds will be in their rooms unless there is a problem. All of the primes have earphones and lenses so that I, and if needed, you, can communicate with them, listen to what is happening, and watch the monitors."

He motioned toward a set of three large monitors, which was labeled from left to right: Cunningham, Witherspoon, Belton.

"If anything goes wrong on a general level, I will likely interfere myself, leaving you in charge of the microphone and monitors. In that case, you will open the box and help everyone follow their instructions. If there are problems with the individuals, we will coach them from here or replace them with their seconds. Do you understand?"

I nodded, terrified.

"The combination for the lock is 1023."

The calm, cool remnants of my ruse were draining slowly out of me, and I stammered something about forgetting my packet although it was already tucked into my jacket. I stumbled blindly into the hallway. The thought of finding Danielle and convincing her not to go through with this insane and arbitrary operation consumed me. I tore open the packet and looked for the information about the hotel. I managed, amid the blur, to find Danielle's room number, and I rushed to her room, pounding on the door.

Danielle opened it. I saw my sister and pushed through her protests into the room. I threw my arms around her and held her for a moment. I grabbed her by the shoulders and looked into her eyes. They were cold and furious.

"Danielle," I said, my voice hoarse, "why are you doing this? Where have you been for the past eleven years? How did you get mixed up in this?"

She pulled away with an impatient jerk.

"I did not get *mixed up in this*, Jack. Monroe is making a man confront his mistakes. Monroe is using his power to create justice and confront an evil that would otherwise go untouched!"

She was shaking with violent pride and began to pace the room. I reached for her arm, but she jerked it wildly out of my grasp.

"Don't you want justice, Jack?" she almost screamed.

"Monroe is going to blackmail this man!" I said angrily. "How is that justice?"

She gave a short scoffing laugh.

"Monroe isn't going to blackmail him, Jack. He's going to make Brown think that he is blackmailing him, then he is going to expose his sin to the world and let the world punish him for who he is, a coward and a liar."

"This is wrong," I said quietly, trying to meet her eyes. She looked away.

"You always think you see things so clearly," she said. "You could never understand..." Her words trailed off for a moment, then she looked at me defiantly.

"You could never have understood why I needed to get away!"

"Is that why you didn't tell me?" I asked accusingly.

"You wouldn't have understood!" she declared again. "I had to go find answers on me own."

"Answers for *what*?"

"For life. About why some bad, cowardly people have it good, and why good...good people don't."

I could hear both of us breathing fast in the silence.

"Mom and Dad?"

"Yes."

"But they weren't killed by bad people. They died accidentally."

She laughed wildly and unnaturally.

"All right, Jack," she said, sardonically. "All right, they died *accidentally*. But Mr. Brown, Mr. Brown did not *accidentally* have an affair. He did not *accidentally* go to great lengths to conceal it, and he did *not* accidentally forget to tell everyone, including his wife, about his folly. *That* was no accident."

"So it's your right to fix it?"

"It's everyone's right!"

"But you are using the same sort of evil to bring about justice for Mr. Brown that you despise in Mr. Brown himself."

"No," she said emphatically. "No, it's not the same."

I stood there looking at her, trying to find her, knowing that Monroe would be waiting for me and that I had very few seconds left and even fewer words.

"No one has the right," I said at last. "Don't do this. It will destroy you."

She looked at me with darkness behind her eyes.

"I've already been destroyed."

I left the room. I felt utterly numb. My mission to save my sister had failed. I could not simply try to save myself without Grey, who was nowhere to be seen, and I could not imagine how to stop the operation itself.

When I reentered Monroe's room, he did not look up. He was intently watching the monitors and talking into the microphone, listening for responses in an earpiece that was barely visible inside his ear. I sat down in an empty chair beside him.

"Cunningham has set up the equipment," he said without looking up. "And Witherspoon is in the room now with Mr. Brown. Everything is going smoothly so far."

I looked at my watch. It was 11:23. In seven minutes, my sister would confront this man, pretend to be his long lost daughter, try to break his heart, remind him of his past, threaten him, destroy his future, and ruin his life. Once she had done it, it could not be undone. Once it was over, it would all be in Monroe's hands, and he would manipulate this man until he had taken everything.

I watched Witherspoon and Mr. Brown's conversation on the monitor, but I could not hear what they were saying. Mr. Brown was a pleasant-looking man. He had fair hair flecked with silver and rather kind eyes. He did not have the sharp, keen look of a typical politician but looked rather more like a father or a teacher. His hands were folded on the table, and he was looking at Witherspoon seriously, the pleasant smile on his face beginning to fade.

I turned away from the monitor, trying not to imagine what Witherspoon was saying.

"Westfield," I heard a pang of anxiety in Monroe's voice as he called my name.

"Westfield, go down and find Belton. She hasn't gone in yet, and it's 11:30. Go see what the matter is *now*."

I hurried down, wondering whether to go to the conference room or Danielle's room, where I had just spoken with her. I wondered wildly if she had changed her mind and run. If she had, I might not ever see her again. It would be nearly impossible for her to hide from Monroe. Fear and hope battled in my chest as I knocked on the door of her room. There was no answer.

I tried the door and found it unlocked. I glanced around the room and saw my sister lying on the bed, apparently sleeping. I saw the glass beside the bed, and with a wrench of horror, I ran to her and listened for sounds of breathing. I held her wrist and felt her pulse. She was only sleeping. She was sleeping deeply and soundly and could not be roused. I stood over her, distressed and confused.

I realized that the pieces had been shattered. I ran down the two flights of stairs to the conference room. As I came around the corner toward the door, Witherspoon caught my arm and held me back.

"It's all right," he assured me. "He's about to go in."

The moment before Lawrence Grey stepped into that room, he looked at me. He held my gaze only for a moment. His eyes held the whole meaning of our adventure, a reply to my silent questions.

Some things cannot be undone. Some things will shatter a person into a thousand unrecognizable pieces, and this was one. I started toward him. He turned away and stepped through the door. It began to close behind him. I reached for the handle as it began to swing out of my grasp with excruciating slowness. I could not speak. I could not breathe. To open it, to enter, to cry out, would be to seal his ruin and mine, but I could not bear to stay silent. Yet in silence I stood, overwhelmed by indescribable despair. The door closed.

PART THREE

The Conspirators

14

I remember standing in front of the door for a long time. In reality, it could not have been very long at all before I heard Stephen Witherspoon's voice behind me.

"Westfield, what are you doing?"

I turned and stared at him. I did not know what I was doing. I had not known for a long time. I thought about this as Witherspoon stared back at me.

"What are you doing here?"

I stared at Witherspoon for a moment, then I turned and walked away from him slowly. He whispered harshly at me to come back, but I ignored him. I walked slowly up the two flights of stairs back to Monroe's room. I entered and he looked up at me, frowning briefly at the open packet in my hand. He quickly turned back to the monitors, too busy for a discussion. I walked up behind him and stared at the monitors over his shoulder.

"They haven't said anything yet," Monroe said, handing me an earpiece. I switched it on and tucked it into my ear. Grey must have taken Danielle's lens and earpiece when he drugged my sister, or even before. He must have been planning this for a while. I wondered how long.

"Must be nerves," Monroe muttered, picking up the microphone. He hesitated then said, "Tell him your story, Grey. Tell him about being raised without a father. You can improvise a little if you have to."

The monitor marked "Cunningham" had been switched to some kind of camera that Claire had set up in the conference room so that we could see Grey's face on that monitor and Mr. Brown's face on Danielle's monitor. Mr. Brown was looking into Grey's face searchingly and sadly. The features of Grey's face were perfectly still for a few moments, then he began to speak.

"I've come to tell you about what my life has been like," he began simply. He paused and stared unseeingly at Mr. Brown. I could not breathe.

"I've lived both in light and in darkness. My mother brought me up with love and kindness, confident that things would turn out for the best. But we also lived in constant fear of losing everything. I learned both to forgive and to distrust. I was never quite sure which was real, the light or the darkness.

"When my mother's wealthy parents provided the funds for me to go to boarding school at the age of twelve, I began experimenting with adopting different personalities according to whatever suited me at the time or benefited me the most. The line between imitation and deceit quickly became blurred when I discovered how easy it was to manipulate people for any purpose that came into my head. Lies became part of the drama, and the pain I caused was collateral damage."

Grey looked at Mr. Brown, out of breath, then continued recklessly.

"In college, I studied philosophy and theatre. I threw myself into both and became proud of my insight into human nature and my power to wield my insight to my own advantage. The way I did this was not always strictly legal. The stakes of the games I was playing were beginning to rise when something happened that shattered the illusion I had created for myself. My mother died."

Mr. Brown gasped and leant forward to speak, but Grey ignored him and continued steadily.

"My mother's death had a strange effect on me. It forced me to confront a power stronger than that of my own intellect. I began to realize that the darkness always seems to overwhelm the light. I abandoned my education and joined a theatre troupe that toured different states and occasionally different countries. In each, I found ways of dabbling in small crimes, mostly for my own amusement.

"Recently, the tour ended, and I got a temporary job working at an office while I figured out my next move. But not many days after that, I was pulled abruptly out of my life and told about the identity of my father, asked if I wanted to confront him. I saw it as the ultimate chance to confront the darkest part of myself, even if it destroyed me.

"I wasn't sure up until a few moments ago whether I would come in here today, if I had enough light left in me to face the darkness. I grew up without a father because a man made a mistake years ago, and I am living proof of the consequences. He has not allowed his mistakes to confine him or allowed his past to influence him until now. He has a choice to make and I have come here to ask him to make it."

Mr. Brown looked at Grey, his eyes red. He reached a hand across the table and their fingers briefly touched. Grey did not seem emotional, only uncomfortable. He shifted a little in his seat and withdrew his hands. His brow contracted and he looked at the table. Mr. Brown put a hand to his eyes.

I looked at Monroe. His fists were clenched and his face was white. He was shaking his head.

"The money, the exposure," he hissed into the microphone. Grey's face did not move.

"The lawyer said that you'd be wanting some money from me?" Mr. Brown broached timidly at last. Grey looked up. His lips were pressed firmly together in an effort to control himself.

"Can you tell me something, Mr. Brown?"

"Anything."

"Why didn't you try to find your long-lost child?"

Monroe leaned forward, picking up the microphone, watching intently. Mr. Brown buried his head in his hands and let out a groan.

"I didn't know I had a child," he said miserably. "I didn't know that your mother was dead. When I told her I was going back, she said she never wanted to see me again, not to try to contact her."

He looked up at Grey, his face contorted with grief. Grey nodded at him and asked, "If you had known that she had had a baby, would you have tried to find her?"

He nodded and said uncertainly, "I think so."

Grey rose from his seat and looked down at Mr. Brown.

"Mr. Brown," he said, "Eleanor Richards is not dead."

I looked at Monroe.

"Is that true?" I asked.

"Of course she's not dead," he snapped at me. "I don't know what he's doing!"

Monroe and I watched dumbly. Mr. Brown looked up at Grey, dumbfounded.

"What do you mean?"

"She's not dead. I can give you her current address if you want to contact her."

Monroe leaned forward. I knew that the address had not been part of the information in Grey's packet.

"Then why—"

Grey walked around the table and put a hand on Mr. Brown's shoulder.

"Eleanor Richards is not dead, but my mother is. She died just after I started college, like I told you."

A few moments of perilous silence passed. Monroe and I held our breath.

"I'm not your son."

Monroe sprang out of his chair, knocking it backward toward me, pacing wildly. He ran back to the screens, and we watched again, riveted.

"I am not your child, Mr. Brown, but I could have been. I was sent here to confront you with your mistakes and I have. But I was also sent here to ruin you, and that I cannot do. I believe that you have been made for a purpose and that more than just yourself would be harmed if I tried to blackmail you. I do not want to see your purpose shattered by your mistakes, but you must not ignore them. You cannot. I know that you want to overcome the past and start anew, but if you do not confront your mistakes, you will regret it forever. Someday it will be too late. It may be too late now. But you must try to make things right."

Mr. Brown stood speechless, nodding.

"As for my story, it is true, but you need not remember it. I recited it for the benefit of another."

Mr. Brown looked bewildered. He seemed about to ask questions. Grey walked toward the door and held it open for Mr. Brown, who passed silently through it. He turned around on the other side and asked, "Who are you?"

Grey looked at him contemplatively for a moment, then replied, "I am Lawrence Fuller."

15

Thinking back on these events, there are details that evade my mind almost entirely. I remember a sound from Monroe and a loud rhythmic thumping that turned out to be my own pulse throbbing in my temples. The air seemed humid. There were beads of sweat on my forehead, and my lungs were constricted. A whir of thoughts, rapid and consecutive, passed through my mind.

A tight grip on my arm arrested me, and I heard Witherspoon's voice in my ear.

"What do you know about this?"

"I don't...I..."

There was no answer forthcoming. I fell into silence. I stared at Monroe. He was pacing around the room again in violent agitation.

"Witherspoon, get out!" he commanded loudly. Witherspoon began to drag me out of the room.

"Leave him."

Witherspoon shot me a furious glance and walked out, shutting the door behind him. Monroe walked over to me, almost running into me and looked into my face.

"You came with him. You knew who he was."

"No!" I cried truthfully. "I didn't."

I was shaking from head to foot.

"You didn't know that he was a Fuller?" he asked earnestly.

"I didn't."

"Where did you come from? Who really sent you here?"

"I—"

"Were you planning this the whole time?"

"No."

Monroe stepped away from me, sitting down in the chair in front of the monitors. His face had drained of all color. I was afraid.

"I didn't know," he said, not to me.

There was a knock at the door. Monroe looked at me. I opened it. Grey walked in and glanced at me.

"I'm sorry about Danielle," he said.

Without waiting for a reply, he walked over to Monroe and stood facing him. I retreated to a corner of the room. They faced each other for a few agonizing seconds, still and silent. My thoughts raced in these seconds. Fuller's voice drifted into my head in bits and pieces. The story he had told me was becoming clearer.

"How did she die?" Monroe asked.

"She contracted an infection. She always had a weak immune system from childhood. It got progressively worse until I was eighteen, and one of her bouts finally got the best of her."

"Did she tell you about me?"

"No, did she tell you about me?"

"No."

A throttled sound came from Monroe.

"I tried to find her. I tried. I didn't know there was a child."

Grey looked at him, his face immobile.

"How did you find out?" Monroe asked at last.

"Daniel Fuller has been keeping track of you ever since your first scheme when you bankrupted him and got him fired. He works for the government now but has been keeping track of you by his own private means. He found me along the way."

"Why did you come here?"

"To confront a man with his biggest mistake."

Monroe nodded.

"Tomorrow, you will take me to see Fuller."

The rest of the day was a strange experience. Monroe hardly spoke a word. I saw no sign of Peter Allen or Katherine Stewart, but as we climbed into a limousine with Monroe, I caught a glimpse of Witherspoon and Claire Cunningham supporting a drowsy Danielle and guiding her into another car.

As we entered the mansion, Monroe said to Grey, "Will you meet me in my study after dinner?"

The simple way he posed the question surprised me. Grey nodded and headed to his room. As I began to follow, Claire Cunningham caught my arm.

"What happened back there? Monroe never cleared me to pick up the footage. He sent Peter and Katherine away. What happened to Danielle?"

I searched my mind for satisfactory answers.

"The plans have changed. Destroy the footage, all right? Take care of Danielle. She's fine, but she'll have a bad headache soon."

Claire studied my face.

"Destroy the footage?"

"Destroy it."

"Why?"

"It won't be useful for exposing Mr. Brown. Things didn't go as planned. Monroe has…decided to shut this one down and let him go."

"Monroe? Let him go?" Claire frowned. Realizing I had nothing to lose, I turned to her.

"Claire, why are you part of the scheme anyway? Don't you feel any kind of guilt for trying to ruin a man's life?"

"Why do you care?"

"I just…I just do."

"It was going to happen anyway…" she said vaguely, her voice trailing off. She was gazing at something over my shoulder. I looked around and saw Witherspoon disappearing behind a half-opened door. I turned back to Claire and she looked at me sadly.

"Stephen thinks that it's good to call people out to face reality."

"What do you think?"

"I don't know. I want to believe that we can change the way things turn out, but I don't know if I believe that we can."

"What if I told you that Mr. Brown doesn't even have a child, that we weren't making him face reality but creating a false reality to torture him?"

Claire stared at me. I turned and went up the stairs and into my room. I sat down on the chair in front of my desk, trying to think about the events that had passed that day, not even daring to guess the events that had yet to occur. The last rays of afternoon sunlight filtered through a slit in the curtains. I felt suddenly weary and sore. A tap sounded on my door.

I opened it and Grey entered. He walked over to the bed and sat down on the edge. His face was drained and drawn as he looked at me.

"I'm sorry about Danielle," he repeated. "I tried to talk her out of going, tried to convince her to let me go instead."

"Where did you get the drugs?"

"Mrs. Harrington's sleeping tablets."

I could not help chuckling a little.

"What's going to happen now?" I asked.

"Monroe wants to talk to me tonight. I came to ask if you would go with me. Tomorrow, we'll go see Fuller. After that, I don't know."

"Of course I'll go."

"Just one more thing, could I have your metal box? I'd like to take a look at a few of the things inside it and take it with us tomorrow."

"Of course. 1023."

I had been carrying it under my jacket and handed it over. I decided for the moment not to say anything about the discoveries I had made about him today and the questions they raised.

Dinner was brief but tedious. Monroe did not appear. No one spoke much.

After dinner, Grey and I walked silently to Monroe's study. Someone had lit a fire in a fireplace that I had not noticed when I sat in the corner on our first day here. The room did not seem as sinister and forbidding but flickered in the tranquil light. Monroe sat in a large armchair and motioned Grey and me to two chairs opposite him.

I thought I could perceive a change in Grey since the first time the blindfolds had been taken off our eyes. He still had the same tousled, intelligent look. He seemed more thin and pale but less frightened. He was haggard but bold.

Monroe, however, had lost his stern, collected expression and instead looked wounded and bewildered. He sat eagerly, leaning forward in his chair, his elbows resting on his knees and his hands tightly clasped. He and Grey regarded one another in this manner for sometime as I sat uneasily, feeling like an intruder. Monroe spoke first.

"Tell me the whole story."

"You've already heard it."

"Tell me more."

"My mother changed her name to Grey before I was born. She never told me much about my father, and I always knew that she didn't want me to ask. For most of my childhood, she taught me herself, but she had to spend a lot of time working. For a long time, I spent most of my days wandering around the town. I had a happy childhood until my mother's parents, whom I had never met, sent me to a boarding school. That's when I realized how different I was. People called me sullen and strange. I began to get into trouble a lot, which no one even knew."

Monroe was listening intently. I thought I saw Grey check himself as his speech grew more fervent. He took a deep breath and leaned back a little in his chair.

"Somehow I managed to get into a university. My mother left me something of an inheritance. I planned to live on it until I found work. The work I found was a little different than I had expected."

"You mentioned crimes."

"Yes."

"What kind?"

"Petty thievery mostly. I reveled in it deeply. When Fuller found me, I had just begun an actual job. I was in between. I still had a taste for risk, which I knew recommended me to his mission. It was not until the night before we came here that he explained the real reason he had chosen me. Before that, the mission of infiltrating a high-class, nameless secret society was more than enough. After he told me that he was my grandfather, I was even more committed."

The silence was suffocating.

"Fuller's been watching me for all these years?"

"Yes."

"And you were pretending to be Grey."

"Technically, I am."

"Why didn't you tell me before?"

"Would it really have stopped you?"

Monroe looked uncomfortable as Grey stared at him intently.

"I don't think it would," Grey said. "You might have shut it down and thrown me out. Blackmailing Mr. Brown gave me the perfect opportunity for the revelation."

Monroe nodded.

"So you never knew about me?" Grey asked after another painful silence.

"No, after Alexis left, I lost contact with her completely."

"Why did you keep doing this after you got your revenge on Fuller?"

"At first, the monetary aspect appealed to me. After my father died, that was irrelevant. But even from the beginning, it was more about the targets themselves. I've never been a materialist nor an absolute narcissist. There's an element of self-gratification in what I do, of course, but I consider myself in the business of justice."

"Not vengeance?"

I shuddered slightly at the harsh word. I thought I caught a hard glint in Monroe's eyes as he looked up.

"Sometimes they are one and the same."

Grey did not reply, but he looked back at Monroe with an expression that was eerily similar.

"What about redemption? Do you believe in it?"

He began to answer but hesitated.

"I do."

"Is that why you want to see Fuller?"

"Yes."

Monroe's face was contrite. Grey's was detached, impenetrable.

"Whether or not there is justice, there are always consequences," he said expressionlessly. He breathed deeply and stood up. Monroe and I stood too. I wished I had not come. Monroe took a step toward Grey and hesitantly rested his hand on Grey's shoulder. Grey stood motionless.

I followed Grey out the door, down the hall, and up the stairs. He went straight into his room and closed the door behind him.

16

When I climbed the ladder to the catwalk, Grey was leaning against the rail a few feet down from me, his head in his hands. As I approached, he looked up at me with an inexpressible look in his eyes.

"I'm sorry, Jack."

I looked back at him quietly.

"I'm sorry that I didn't tell you all this from the beginning."

"You could have."

"I didn't know what I was going to do until yesterday."

"You could have told me you were his son."

"I didn't want to tell you unless it was necessary."

"Why?"

He turned and looked at me, his face rigid.

"He's a villain," he said, his words sharp in the cold air. "We were sent here to defeat him, and I just want to save him. He's my father, whatever that means. He's a villain. And you expected me to tell you I was his son? I could hardly tell myself."

"But it is true?"

His jaw worked. I wished I had not said it.

"What I mean is you were supposed to be Mr. Brown's long lost child, a child that apparently never existed. I just wondered if you were using the idea, turning it on Monroe. You successfully thwarted the operation and kept us safe, at least for the time being."

I cringed inwardly at the mistrust in my words. Grey turned and grasped the rails. His knuckles were white.

"So you're wondering if the game is over yet."

"I had to ask."

"It's not a bad idea, of course."

I remained silent. He sighed.

"I was not lying. You may believe that with whatever degree of trust you have in me."

I breathed in the night air and closed my eyes.

"I believe you."

I did believe him, but I still could not take it in.

"So Fuller really is your grandfather?"

"Yes."

"It almost makes sense out of everything. Why he has been tracking Monroe for all these years, why he wanted us to stop him but didn't seem interested in sending him to the law."

He nodded.

"Do you think we succeeded?"

"I think we've stopped him, at least for now. I don't know if we can save him."

He bent his head. I slowly raised my hand and put it on his shoulder. We stood together for a few minutes, quietly taking in the events of the day and trying to prepare ourselves for whatever was to come.

The night was long and uneventful. I awoke with the feeling that I had been drained dry. I rose, dressed, combed my hair, and looked at myself in the mirror. I thought I looked older, paler, my eyes keener, and my cheeks more hollow. I hardly recognized myself.

I met Grey in the hall outside our rooms, and we went downstairs together. He looked much the same as I did, although perhaps for once not quite as calm. I knew as we walked down the stairs that we would not be going back up. Monroe met us in the entrance room, and we all went out to the limousine.

Our ride from the mansion to the faceless gray building was tense and solemn. I looked out the window, taking refuge in the outside world as a safeguard from the terrors within. The sky seemed strangely dark for this time of morning.

At last, we pulled up to the bleak building that had formed the backdrop of my first acquaintance with Grey. Monroe's face was motionless. He showed no flicker of fear or surprise as we approached the doors, followed by Hart, whose presence seemed to go unnoticed by the other two.

We walked down the now-familiar hallways to the large, metal double doors that led to the room where Grey and I had been held captive in the days before we were given our mission. It was not without a sense of dread that I entered them again.

The room was lit dimly. Across from us, almost exactly in the center of the room, Daniel Fuller sat behind a large wooden desk, dressed in a suit, his hands folded on the surface of the desk. The light was coming from two lamps on either side of his desk. Three chairs sat in front of it. They looked inviting, almost comically incongruous with the occasion. The vast room was otherwise empty. The door slammed. The three of us stood for a few moments in the corner of the room. Then Monroe stepped forward boldly and strode across the room toward Fuller. Grey and I followed. Monroe began to look more like himself, his head thrown back, his arms swinging at his sides.

Monroe centered himself in front of Fuller's desk, planting his feet shoulder-width apart and letting his arms hang by his sides, his hands in loose fists. Fuller smiled at him, and neither took his eyes off the other as Fuller said, "Won't you sit down, Felix?"

"I'll stand."

Fuller broke his gaze and looked at us as we stood warily behind Monroe.

"Lawrence, Jack, have a seat."

We sat down in two chairs beside Monroe.

"So you have found out about me," Fuller said after a long silence.

"I have known about you and what you've been doing for a long time," Monroe said drily. If this announcement surprised Fuller, he made no sign of it.

"I see," he said simply. "And now you've come to see me."

"You have finally successfully thwarted one of my schemes."

Fuller smiled slowly.

"It was not I who thwarted you. It was my agents."

"Your agents," Monroe scoffed. "You mean your minions? Did you 'recruit' them in the same way you've recruited others?"

"I did."

"My agents, at least, are willing to be part of my operations. In fact, they are more than exceptionally eager."

"That is the way of the world, isn't it?" Fuller commented, unruffled. "People are much more eager to see what kind of trouble they can stir up than to try to stop it."

"Stir up trouble?"

Grey and I exchanged glances. Monroe was getting angry. He was not the calm, almost contrite man he had been last night. Perhaps they had been enemies for too long, and the antipathy between them was too deeply ingrained to let go of now. Perhaps I should have known what was going to happen next.

Fuller stood up behind his desk, and the two men faced each other.

"To stir up trouble," Fuller repeated. "To destroy the lives of innocent people—"

"Innocent?"

"I know that you never invent their crimes. You exploit their weaknesses. You think that no one is innocent in the true sense of the word, and I cannot disagree with you."

A triumphant smile flitted across Monroe's face.

"We are all stained by the guilt and shame of our mistakes," Fuller continued. "But it is those I call innocent who have had the courage to stand back up and move forward, only to have you knock them down again. You could do so much good, Felix. You have so much power, so many resources. You have always had a deep understanding of human beings, but instead of having compassion on them, accepting their faults and weaknesses, you sit in your mansion, trying to purge the evils of the world by taking justice into your hands. But you will never feel satisfied that you have done it. You cannot purify evil. You can only create more evil by choosing to exact justice instead of to grant mercy. Ruthless revenge is not for you to take. It is your duty only to forgive those who have wronged you and to help those who seek redemption to find it if you can."

There was a long silence after Fuller's speech.

"You are a bitter old man."

Monroe broke the silence with a deadly voice.

"You are bitter because I exacted justice from *you*. You took my goodness from me when you took the greatest good I ever had. You took Alexis from me, and now I find out you took my child. You destroyed me and I destroyed you. Now you want to destroy me again. We are the same, you and I. You say I take the law into my own hands, so do you. What else have you done with the system you've created here? Haven't you poured so much of your energy into avenging yourself against me that you sent your own grandson into my house to risk his life and to take part in my schemes that you find so despicable?"

Monroe's breathing was coming hard and fast.

"You and I are the same man on opposite teams. You hide behind your morality. You think you are the hand of justice. But you are only another man who thinks he knows how the world should be run and that he is powerful enough to try to run it. You do not know all or see all. You think everyone can be redeemed. You are blind to the true evils of the world. You are blind to the suffering."

"I do believe that everyone can be redeemed. But I do not believe that everyone will be. I know that there is evil in the world, and I know of suffering. But I believe that the evil and suffering has a purpose, that redemption is possible, necessary to justify the evils you speak of."

Monroe gave a short laugh. Then his grim, terrifying smile faded, and his face became totally white. He quivered with rage. Fuller watched him with quiet eyes, looking grave and almost sad.

"Why have you come here, Felix?" he said quietly, prompting. "You could have seen me before. Why come now?"

"After all these years…" Monroe began and broke off, his voice trembling. His hands, clenched tightly into fists by his sides, were shaking violently.

"After nineteen years, I learn that the woman I loved is dead, gone forever. And I was never able to find her. I learn that I have a son who is utterly estranged from me. I watch him come into my house to destroy me, sent by you."

Fuller did not say a word. Monroe continued, "Many years ago, I swore to destroy you. I thwarted your dealings with my father, bankrupted you, ruined you, took everything you had. But no, not everything. I wanted to see your suffering. And I saw you suffer but not as I had suffered. I saw you lose everything but not what I had lost. You took my love from me and emptied my life. It was you and you alone who showed me the cruelties of the world, and now you blame me for believing in them. It was you who first showed me injustice, and now you blame me for claiming justice for myself, for claiming vengeance. Well, I have come here today to end you at last, to destroy you forever. I do not believe in good. I do not believe in God. I believe only in myself and what I can do."

His words, spoken in a high, strained tone, ended. There was a rush of movement, and before a moment could pass, his arm was outstretched, a gun in his hand, a look of pure hatred on his face. With a shock, I saw that Grey was on his feet, his arm extended toward Monroe with a small pistol pointed at his head.

There was an instant of wildly charged stillness. Fuller looked from Monroe to Grey and Monroe looked from Fuller to Grey in surprise.

"Where did you get that?" I asked under my breath.

"Your box."

"Well, well," Monroe said smirking, "how resourceful."

"You had us pick them up yourself."

"Like father like son, I suppose. Never come unprepared."

Fuller was shaking his head at Grey, whose eyes were fixed steadily on Monroe.

"I am not like you," he said.

Monroe laughed.

"We're all conspirators here."

Then with hardly a movement, he pulled the trigger. Two shots sounded as one.

17

Time froze after the shots had been fired. Grey dropped his gun and grabbed my arm, and I remember feeling the tightness of his fingers around my sleeve. There was a tingling sensation at the back of my neck as if I were being burned. My gaze was fixed on Monroe. His eyes were blasting with rage, the eyes of a man who would not be swayed by man or nature.

I found myself thinking about sitting in the tree house after my parents had died and thinking about how cruel it was that an accident had killed them, that if it had been a man, I could have found him and avenged their death. I understood Monroe's vengeance, and I despaired in understanding.

These thoughts slowly drifted through my mind in the moment when the bullet was travelling through the air toward Fuller. He hit the ground instantly. Everything that happened afterward happened quickly. Monroe clutched at his hand, staring at the blood that seeped from between his fingers. Grey dropped his grip on my arm and ran to Fuller's side. Monroe looked at Fuller and then began to run, or maybe only stride, out of the room. I stood paralyzed for too long before realizing that I ought to run after him.

I arrived at the doors of the building just in time to grab Monroe's arm and jerk him back for a moment. I planted myself between him and the door, hardly knowing what I was doing. He looked at me almost reluctantly.

"Don't," he commanded with wild sanity.

I stood my ground.

"I like you, Jack, but you can't stop me from leaving."

I was breathing hard. I shook my head. He raised his gun and pointed it at my head. My mind was blank.

I heard a shot. My knees buckled. My head hit the concrete of the steps. As my eyes closed, I saw Monroe open the door to his car, revealing Witherspoon and Claire. Claire glanced back apologetically before closing the door. I shuddered violently and everything went black.

───◆◆◆───

These are the events that transpired while I lay unconsciously on the steps of the building, as Grey later related them to me:

While I lay unconsciously on the steps of the building, Grey was at Fuller's side, examining the wound in his chest and trying to stop the bleeding. He called out but no one heard him. Fuller did not last long.

Grey managed to get Fuller's head into his lap and talked to him in a panic, trying to keep him awake. At last, Fuller quieted him and began to speak.

"I am sorry that I did not know you better. I am sorry that I ever sent you into Monroe's mansion—"

"No, I was willing to go."

"Not until I convinced you."

Grey smiled weakly.

"All my life, I hoped that I'd be found," Grey said. "I always knew that I'd been lost. When my mother died, I felt that I had been lost all over again. But you found me. You found me and told me who I was and what I was supposed to do. You told me what I was made for. Now I know."

"Lawrence," Fuller said, his eyes bright, "do you know why I sent you?"

"To save him."

"I thought you would remind him. He has always been lost too. My daughter tried to find him, but I knew he was only ever going to hurt her. He was going to take her into the darkness. At least, I thought I saw. I thought that you could help him now. I am sorry that I have caused you pain."

Grey shook his head.

"One last thing."

Grey leaned toward Fuller's face and looked into his eyes. He reached up a feeble hand to touch the boy's head.

"It's never too late for redemption, Lawrence. Keep fighting for it. Do not forget that you were found."

Grey nodded wordlessly. They passed their last moments together. A little while later, Grey found me lying on the steps outside the building, unconscious in a small pool of blood.

———◆◆◆———

I opened my eyes and squinted at a very bright light. It looked like the afterlife, but it did not smell like it. It was a smell I recognized. I closed my eyes. It smelled like fear and pain. I was in a hospital. I stretched out my hand and felt the thin, crisp sheets. I tried to sit up, but my head was pounding. My left leg throbbed with pain. I groaned.

A nurse approached my bedside and smiled gently at me.

"Good morning, young man."

This time, I managed to open my eyes all the way.

"Good morning. Where am I?"

"You're in a hospital," she said kindly. "You've been unconscious for two days. You had a nasty concussion on the back of your head, but you're going to be all right."

"My leg—"

"Yes. It was shot. It's going to take a while to recover, and you may be limping for quite some time, but you're going to be all right."

I dimly took in what she was saying and nodded, hoping that she would go away so that I could think a little more clearly. My head was pounding.

She did go away, and I lay on the hospital bed for a few hours, trying to remember everything that had happened to me and speculating about what was going to happen next. The mission was over. I wondered where Monroe had gone and where Grey and Hart were. Monroe must be in hiding, I thought. He would not show his face directly after a murder that had two witnesses. I determined that it must have been Grey who brought me to the hospital, so he would probably come back eventually to check on my recovery.

After a few hours, Grey did visit me. He told me about Fuller's death and Monroe's disappearance. He and Hart had been trying to sort out Fuller's affairs for the past two days while they waited for me to wake up. He sat down by my bedside and pulled his chair up to the edge of the bed. He rested his elbows on the railing of the bed.

"Jack," he began, "you know that Fuller was the head of an organization."

"Yes."

"They track, locate, and anticipate crime. They strategize to prevent it, often sending in agents to do work similar to what you and I did. It's all unofficially sanctioned by the government."

"What does this have to do with me?"

"Fuller wanted you to join it permanently."

I took a deep breath and looked at the ceiling, a sinking feeling in my stomach. I thought about the uncertain life I had been living for the past days and what it would be like to live like that forever. I thought about going back to sleep.

"You want to drag me into another adventure?"

He smiled roguishly, a twinkle in his eye that I had not seen before.

"I understand why he would plan to hand this organization over to you, but why did he want me to join?"

Grey looked at me seriously.

"It seems that he had a special connection with Jonathan and Amy Westfield."

My heart skipped a beat.

"How did he know my parents?"

"That is a long story that I have not pieced together yet."

"My parents, were they—"

"Agents? It seems that they were."

My head fell back onto the pillow. My life was changing rapidly in retrospect. Many confusing moments of my childhood rushed to my mind: the stays with aunts and uncles, neighbors, and grandparents; the confusion about what my father did for a living; my mother sitting up at night, waiting for him to come home. I thought about their car accident and wondered if I had gotten the whole story. I wondered why Fuller had not told me this from the beginning.

"If you're in, I'm in," I said.

"Just like before?"

"Just like before."

"Our lives have changed a lot in the past week, haven't they, Jack?"

"They have."

ACKNOWLEDGMENTS

My parents are the first people who told me I could write and they have never stopped believing in me. Thank you for raising me, teaching me, and supporting me all along the way.

Dr. Dougherty, you were a vital component in the conception and criticism of this story when it was only an undergraduate thesis. You were the first professor I had who told me I could write. I will never forget it. Thank you for your honesty.

Dr. Garrett, being in your class has put an indelible mark on my identity as a writer. Thank you for your unique combination of wisdom, warnings, and encouragement.

Lauren, thank you for the hours spent in the coffee shop responding to my pestering questions and surmises with thoughtful ideas and, when necessary, gentle mockery.

Carly, your ability never to doubt me has been a foundation on which to stand. Ever since you listened to my poetry in the mobile home, I knew I could count on you as a fan and a friend. You always know what I need to hear, even when I don't want to hear it.

This book would not exist without Tate Publishing, and I am especially thankful to my project manager Kate Reynolds for helping me through the process.

Ryan, you believed in me for the both of us. You pushed me toward my dreams with unrelenting vigor and I could not have done any of this without you. Thank you for being my best friend, my critic, and my biggest fan.

"I've finally found some answers to a few of the questions that have riddled me all my life."

I sighed.

"I have more unresolved questions than ever."

He sat by my bed for the rest of the evening. We conversed intermittently but spent most of the time in companionable silence. I could never have fathomed the way my life was going to change when I was knocked unconscious the first night of my adventure. To this day, as I sit at my desk writing this story, reflecting on all of the things I have seen and done, I think that the moment that changed my life the most was the moment I met Lawrence Grey.